BATTLE OF WILLIAM'S HILL

BOOK 2 OF THE WARS OF WRETEN

DAN HOPKINS

THE BATTLE OF WILLIAM'S HILL

THE WARS OF WRETEN BOOK 2

DAN HOPKINS

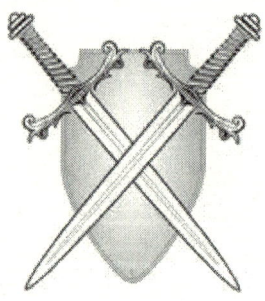

CONTENTS

MAP OF WRETON 1
CHAPTER 1 2
CHAPTER 2 8
CHAPTER 3 14
CHAPTER 4 21
CHAPTER 5 28
CHAPTER 6 39
CHAPTER 7 46
CHAPTER 8 53
CHAPTER 9 59
CHAPTER 10 72
CHAPTER 11 75
CHAPTER 12 81
CHAPTER 13 90
CHAPTER 14 96
CHAPTER 15 100
CHAPTER 16 106
CHAPTER 17 122
CHAPTER 18 130
CHAPTER 19 139
CHAPTER 20 144
CHAPTER 21 150
CHAPTER 22 160
CHAPTER 23 168
CHAPTER 24 174
CHAPTER 25 182
CHAPTER 26 188

CHAPTER 27	197
CHAPTER 28	202
CHAPTER 29	215
CHAPTER 30	221
CHAPTER 31	226
CHAPTER 32	232
ALSO BY DAN HOPKINS	239
ACKNOWLEDGMENTS	240
ABOUT THE AUTHOR	241

To my good friend Shane,
I look forward to our next family trip to Mexico.

MAP OF WRETON

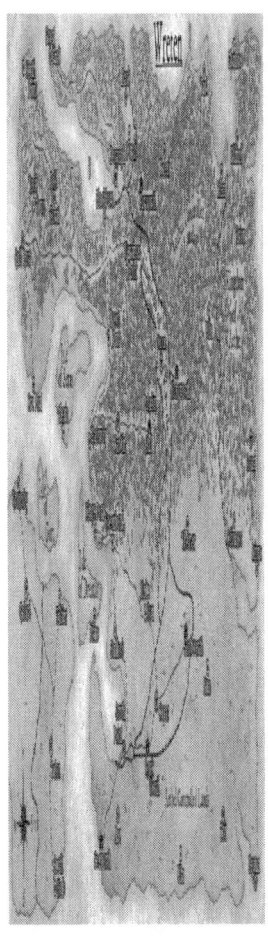

1

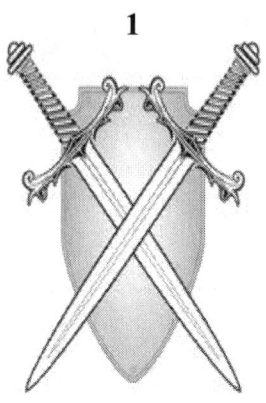

"I hate snow." Twenty-two-year-old Eric Bowman muttered as he swiped at the freshly fallen flakes off his cloak. "I swear it makes everything we do all the harder!" Tightening his cloak, he repositioned himself in the saddle, glancing down at the horse he loved so much and patting her gently on the neck. She had proven her worth many times during this quest.

"This isn't so bad. You spent too much time in the scorching deserts of the far south, boy." Eric's uncle, Samuel Bowman, accused. "I need to toughen you up again." He let out a hearty laugh.

Samuel was an old soldier of forty-one years with two crowns tattooed under his eye, a mark of honor given to veterans of the king's army. One tattoo is granted after each term of service.

"I think the fighting we've done the past months has shown I'm tough enough for this weather," Eric challenged.

"You don't hear me complaining, do you?" His uncle hollered back.

Eric scoffed, knowing Samuel was trying to get under his skin. "Old man, maybe we should climb down off these horses, and I'll show you what I can do! Rub your face with fresh snow in front of all these women watching."

Samuel laughed again, considering all he'd seen his nephew do with the speed and strength the brother gods, Boreal and Balent, had gifted him with. Samuel peered up at the early morning sky and the green moon the scriptures said the brothers lived on. "I've earned my ink twice, boy. Think you can take me on?"

Eric chuckled. "I wouldn't want to get you all wet. Those old bones of yours can't handle the cold anymore."

"Thanks be to the brothers. We've seen you kill and know just how deadly you are, lad. I will not pretend to understand all the magic I've seen." Samuel smiled proudly at his nephew. "I still have a hard time wrapping my thick head around the workings of the brothers and how we ended up way up here in the north with friendly Elves."

"The brothers work in strange ways," Eric agreed, turning his head to the front of the column where he could see Prince Duncan Goodwin, the Crown Prince of Stalwart, riding alongside his squire, Brandon.

Stalwart was the strongest nation in the coalition of kingdoms united against the Druid Elves and the Empire of Aethel. The two sides had been at war for hundreds of years.

Prince Duncan, who had spent his life sickly, unknowingly cursed by the Druids, could not be the warrior he wished and was expected to be. He'd long since been nicknamed the Sickling Princeling. To Duncan's shame, he could not earn his ink or even train to be a soldier. After Lirdjss murdered Prince Simon and used his blood in a dark magical ritual, increasing her powers, Duncan learned their family was directly descended from the gods. That night, the brothers had weakened the curse on Duncan, giving him back his strength, and the prince found himself on a quest to find the light Elves to eradicate the scourge.

Using Prince Simon in visions, the brothers guided Duncan to Eric, who had been granted gifts from the brothers many years ago. Together, Duncan and Eric travelled north into Dwarven lands with a

Dwarf of noble birth named Berar, the prince's personal guard, Davy Talltree, Brandon, an orphan squire, and Eric's uncle, Samuel. Many others in their party did not survive when they were forced to fight off several attacks by Trolls and Vandian warriors, a tribe of bloodthirsty humans who had allied with the Druids centuries ago.

A large Vandian force had besieged the light Elves and Duncan's party in an old, abandoned city. Duncan had used his newly found magical powers to help them escape, only to be saved by a Dwarven army led by Berar's brother, Grilrig. Grilrig relinquished his title and granted the right and title of clan lord back to Berar to avoid an uprising amongst the Ironblade clan.

Eric stared ahead at Prince Duncan and saw his love Inda riding alongside him, talking of magic, he guessed.

Inda was the sister of Lirdjss and the daughter of the Elven emperor. She denounced the dark Druid magic and ran away, finding many other Elves hiding in secret, known only to a few in Stalwart and the Dwarf hierarchy. Once Eric and his band arrived, Inda and her followers removed Prince Duncan's curse and taught him how to use his newly found powers properly.

"Stop staring at your girl!" Samuel barked, trying to make him feel uncomfortable.

"I can't," Eric replied. Red-faced, he glanced back at her with her soft pale skin and long blond hair. He smiled and wished he could lie by a fire wrapped in a blanket of furs with her. "I do not know what I would do without her."

"You're certainly happier since you met her," Samuel said. "Funny, though."

"How do you mean?"

"Well, you hated the entire Elf race with a passion only a few short months ago and would have killed any of them on sight."

Eric grinned.

"I never knew there were good Elves in the world, or ones this pretty." He glanced over his shoulder at the long trail of Dwarven cavalry sitting proudly on their mountain goats and infantry, carefully positioned around the Vandian prisoners. He peered farther back at the hundreds of human and Elf civilians who followed the column south from their home, looking for safety.

"This march south to Berar's lands will take much too long with the prisoners," Eric said with disappointment.

"I know, but once we get to Durgh, the Dwarves will take the weight off." Samuel replied, "I am hoping his people will have a feast prepared."

Eric laughed. "A new clan lord coming home, I would expect nothing less."

2

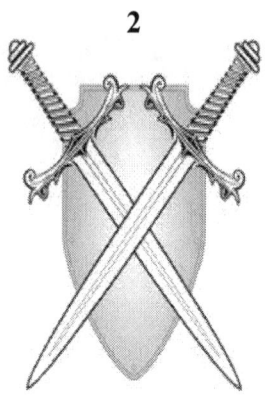

The entire column arrived at Durgh without incident, save the disappearance of twenty of the previous clan lords, former guards. Not much was said about it, as most simply assumed they had deserted.

Eric let out a sigh of relief once there they all inside the safety of the city walls. He glimpsed back and saw everyone else had relaxed as well.

Berar's homecoming was a spectacle to see. Thousands of the city's inhabitants lined the streets and waved at their clan lord. Many wept with joy as he rode by, heading up the steps to the mountain stronghold. Standing under the massive statue of the Stone Kin, he turned, letting his people see him. Taking his axe from the strap on his back, Berar held it high over his head and let them cheer him. He said nothing and waved, smiling. Some of his people tossed rings of iron to him, a Dwarven sign of respect from the old times. He picked up several of the rings, sliding them onto his fingers, leaving the rest for his men to gather, and thanked everyone who made the offering.

The people were not happy about Inda, and her armed Elves following the clan lord inside the gates. Some of the Dwarven population cried out in shock at first. Dofic, an old, respected Elf who had come north with the Dwarf army and other important nobles, kept the peace. At least until a few hundred Vandian prisoners were marched in, bound with chains. Durgh's population had exploded, with Dwarf refugees running from the Vandian horde that raided villages and towns and killed so many. The city's folk began throwing trash, rocks, pieces of firewood. An old Dwarf, who had lost all his family to the horde, attacked one with a dagger. Eric pulled him off the bleeding Vandian. He held the old Dwarf as he cried in his arms.

"I do not know why we are keeping these dogs alive!" Davy Talltree muttered as he watched them march by, chained together and pelted with anything people could get their hands on. Several Vandians had died from injuries until Berar's troops restored order.

Late in the evening, Berar called everyone to his throne room. They were escorted in at once, and when they arrived, they found Berar seated at the same large table they had eaten at the last time they were in the room.

Eric could hardly recognize his friend Berar. He had lost his old clothes and dirty armor everyone had gotten used to seeing him in and was wearing a fine dark brown woolen shirt and leather pants to match. He had a sheepskin cloak over his shoulders, which he pulled off as soon as he saw them walk in, and the gold and iron band wrapped around his head had the crest of Clan Ironblade.

Berar was alone except for two of the young Elf Calrith's warriors who stood back, watching every move.

"Good, Berar is taking no chances with his brother still alive." Eric smiled, leaning into Samuel.

"Smart," Samuel nodded.

Berar stood from the table and greeted everyone like old friends. Brandon stopped and gazed upward at the giant chandeliers. His attention was taken by the paintings on the walls, and he explored the room. The room was kept bright by dozens of candles and lamps hung on the walls.

"Come, my old friends, I have food coming for all of us," Berar shouted excitedly as Dofic entered the room and sat near the head of the table. Prince Duncan sat directly across from Berar. Eric and Inda sat beside each other, holding hands under the table.

The finest ale was brought in with wine for whoever wanted some. Eric grinned at how happy Berar was.

"Did you see your mother?" Eric asked.

Berar roared with laughter. "I did, and she is pleased I didn't end my brother's life. She insisted on making us this meal. Wait until you taste her pork sausage and peppers." Berar leaned over toward Inda, and whispered, "No worries, my dear, I told them to make something without meat for you and yours."

Berar waited a moment and let everyone relax and get used to the room. "I am going to get right to business now before we eat and drink too much—"

Samuel interrupted, "Let me guess, you want your pay for the work you did for me."

The room burst into laughter. Berar returned the joke with another, took a long drink of his ale, and grew serious once more.

"I am wondering how quickly you will move south again?"

Everyone stared at Duncan and Eric.

"As soon as possible, I'm afraid. We will go directly to Warrior's Point to meet my father's army. He has called for everyone to gather there," Duncan answered.

"Yes, we will." Eric nodded.

Berar dropped his head in disappointment. "I was hoping to come with you. Unfortunately, I am required here. The raids from the Vandians and the Elf armies have caused a disaster, and they are still out there, looking for you, Prince Duncan. I cannot leave with you until my people are safe. I will ride out to meet them." His voice held genuine disappointment. "I've arranged for anyone who wishes to stay, whether it be Elf or human, will be welcome and safe."

Inda sighed in relief. "Thank you, Lord Berar. I was wondering where we could settle them."

"I think it would be best to leave them all here. I'd wager armed Elves wouldn't be accepted at Warriors Point right now," Eric said.

"Point made." Gelvyr, the light Elf guard commander, nodded to Eric.

"No!" Duncan said sharply. "We will take some Elves with us. We will show my father and all of Wreten there are good Elves, and we can co-exist with them."

"Maybe Prince Duncan is right. Maybe you should bring a few hundred of the warriors with you. I could sure use some archers, though, if they want to help clear out my lands."

Gelvyr smiled. "Calrith can help you with that, and my warriors would gladly assist you in defense of your land."

"Perfect." Berar replied, "Let them know they will earn a fair wage." He turned back to Eric and Duncan. "How many Elves do you wish to take?"

"Two hundred. Mounted only, please, so we can move faster. Moving with speed is something I learned from an Outrider. It makes it harder for them to find us." Duncan winked at Eric.

"Very well. I will also provide two hundred of my ram riders to escort you to the border. It should be safe from that point on."

"I agree. Thank you, Lord Berar."

"It was my honor to fight with you, Prince Duncan. I wish I was coming with you." Berar grinned.

"Until the day we ride into battle as brothers once again." Eric raised his goblet of ale to Berar.

3

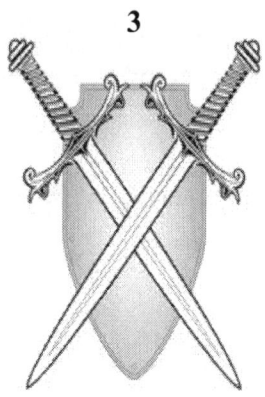

Nine days of hard riding had passed since they left Durgh and their friend the clan lord. They passed by the Dwarven king's city of Dorgagh without stopping, choosing to ride hard to Duncan's father at Warriors Point. They had been delayed by Dwarf patrols many times when they had realized there were Elves in the party who were armed and mounted.

Berar had sent his brother Grilrig, the former clan lord, along with the Dwarf contingent. Grilrig was forced to show documents with his brother's seal, authorizing the Elves to be moved through Dwarven lands. Grilrig cringed every time he had to speak to Dwarf commanders about the odd situation. To make things worse, many had not heard of his demotion.

They were still two days' hard march from the Stalwart border when they met up with hundreds of human Elf hunters answering King William's call for the veterans to return to service, heading south to meet the army. This caused more than a few tense situations when they saw the armed Elf warriors in the column, but it always worked out well in the end, and most joined them on their journey. Eric and Duncan were pleased as their ranks increased with men who knew how to fight and would not shy away from one. It made Eric feel better for the safety of Duncan if they ran into an Aethel unit, but just in case, he always made sure the Elf contingent was camped well away from the hunters with the Dwarves between them.

"We will be at the border soon," Grilrig informed Eric as they rode side by side down the stone-paved highway. Inda was behind him, speaking with Duncan about magic he knew nothing about.

"Yes, a few more days. Warriors Point is still a long way, though," Eric said.

"I've never been there, though I've always wanted to see it," Grilrig said with a touch of disappointment. "I've heard there is no better place for drinking and a good tavern brawl."

"We'll be there soon enough. This war will not end tomorrow, and I'm sure there will be a Dwarf contingent again attached to the King's army." Eric assured him.

"Yes." Grilrig agreed. "I am sure Berar will have me with it. I'm sure he would never sleep well with me at home just down the hall."

Eric stared at him and asked, "Can you blame him?"

Grilrig shook his head. "No." He dropped his head in shame, trying to make it look his attention was on his ram, and patted its heavy thick muscle-bound neck. "I do not think I will go home again."

Eric studied him and wondered where Grilrig was going with this. He understood the Dwarf would never be accepted at home again.

"Where do you want to go?"

"With you," he said without hesitation.

This surprised Eric as he listened to the Dwarf speak.

"I am a good soldier. You have seen that."

Eric nodded.

"When I was younger, I fought at the clan towers and helped keep the Elves away. The only chance I will get to come home again is if I win some glory and be recognized as a great warrior."

Eric considered this. "You can fight Grilrig. And you can lead. I saw that when you stepped in to assist us against the Vandians at Dard." He watched as the

Dwarf's shoulders tightened. "I would be pleased to have you with us, as long as Prince Duncan agrees."

Grilrig laughed. "You will not regret this, Eric, I promise."

Inda could be heard sucking in a deep breath, her hand coming to rest on her chest. She gaped at Duncan. "Do you feel that?"

"There is a Druid nearby, a strong one. We can feel it! If we can feel him, you can bet the Druid can feel us as well." Duncan's gaze meeting Eric's as his body stiffened and fear flashed across his face.

Four Dwarf riders rounded the corner on the road that edged the mountainside. The one in the lead was calling out something in his native tongue. Eric watched Grilrig, who shook his head. "Elf cavalry Eric, lots of them, less than two miles out."

Eric surveyed the area, realizing the ground they were on was not suitable for fighting. He was about to suggest fleeing, but the Dwarf rams would never outrun the enemy horses. He regarded Grilrig. "Do you know this area?"

The Dwarf nodded. "If you are looking for a place to fight, we need to head up." He raised his hand and pointed at the mountain.

Eric followed his direction, seeing what he was talking about. High above them, there was a sizeable snow-covered piece of ground with a long, gentle slope. Gelvyr was nearby and shouted agreement.

"Up the mountain! We go up!" Eric wasted no time. He spurred his horse, and they rounded the corner, galloping to where the cliff ended, and the trees were growing against the road. He turned his horse and spurred her hard. She grunted in protest, but dug her hooves in deep and forced herself up the mountain.

After a brief time of ascending the mountain face, Eric glanced behind him. He could already see the enemy cavalry galloping down the road after them. He could see their force would be much larger than his, and he pushed his horse harder.

The Dwarves on their rams were already far up the mountainside. The rams were much more suited for the terrain. Inda and Duncan were right behind Eric, followed by his Elf contingent and those who had joined them.

Eric's horse was breathing heavily, but she continued to press on, and soon they reached the snow line where the slope of the mountain eased dramatically, allowing the horses to breathe again, but then the snow quickly deepened, and they were forced to get off their mounts and lead them on foot.

Eric cursed Grilrig and shouted at him for what he saw as a bad idea. Grilrig laughed at him and called back, "This is my country outrider, and this is my type of fighting! You will see."

Eric did not answer him and just kept pulling on the horse's reins while he stumbled in knee-deep snow. He observed Inda and saw her struggling as well, but keeping up.

Finally, they reached the spot where the Dwarves had already formed up with their backs against a cliff wall that was almost straight up. Eric contemplated the situation and shouted again, "Grilrig! We are trapped here!"

"Yes," Grilrig replied with a laugh. "But their horses cannot walk in this snow either." Eric stared at the ground they had just crossed as he panted, trying to catch his breath. He saw three hundred yards of open land with no cover. If they wanted them, the Elves would have to cross it on foot or clumsily on horseback. He looked to his left and saw the Elf hunters stringing their bows, and to his right, the warriors doing the same. Some Dwarves had crossbows. They were readying as well. Eric knew his numbers were just over four hundred.

"I hope you two can stop this Druid. How strong is it?" Eric asked Duncan and Inda.

"I believe it is one that killed my brother," Duncan called, his face twisted with anger.

"I'm sure of it. With the god's blood, the Druid will be much stronger than me," Inda said.

"Not me!" Duncan said. He was itching for a fight. Eric nodded at the prince. "We will try to leave the Druid for you then."

As they waited, the first Elf cavalries crested the mountainside entering the snow and took position on the flat, just out of range of the allied bows. More and more enemies came up over the edge of the mountain onto the flat. Eric estimated he was looking at well over a thousand enemies. He regarded Duncan. "That's a whole lot of trouble."

4

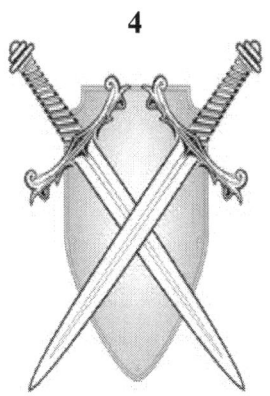

The Elf cavalry was forced to dismount, just as Eric had to do with his own horse. Their leader kept them back out of range from Eric's archers. He watched as they lined up with their short shields tightly together, trying to form a shield wall while pointing lances forward, and waited.

After several minutes, Samuel walked over beside Eric and placed a hand on his nephew's shoulder. "If they were infantry, I am sure they would have advanced on us by now." Samuel studied the enemy and wondered why. After a moment, he continued, "I would bet they are afraid of our archers, their shields are smaller than their infantry shields, and they can't protect them as well."

"Probably something with that." Eric replied, "My bet is they are afraid of Duncan."

Samuel grinned at his nephew abashedly. "Yeah, I guess that would make more sense." He walked back down the line to his former position.

Inda stood overlooking the hundreds of Elf fighters they would soon fight. "I hoped to never see that red and black armor again." She took several steps closer and scrutinized them, trying to figure out who the Druid was. "I can still feel him," she whispered. "It is like I can feel the cold emotions. He has no empathy for us."

"I feel him as well, Inda, I feel him, and I think I've met him before." Duncan wrapped himself in his cloak while staring at the Elves.

"When? Where?"

Eric watched as Duncan placed a hand on his forehead, closing his eyes. Inda did the same, finding their light. Both opened their eyes quickly and gasped. Duncan looked at Eric and shouted, "It's the one who led the attack at your family home!"

"Oh, come on!" Eric growled in disbelief. "Out here?"

"Yes!" Duncan snapped back.

Eric turned to his enemy and shook his head, and whispered, "What are the odds of that?" He turned to

Inda. "How well can you fair against one of these Druids?"

"Not well. I can help Duncan, but he will be the one that will have to do most of the spell casting." She looked at the enemy line again. "He seems so angry, and he knows I am here with you, Duncan, and that has made him even more bloodthirsty. He wants to kill me. I can feel it."

"So, can I." Duncan agreed.

Eric grew angry. Inda was the one he intended to spend his life with, and this Druid, wanting to kill her, was not in his plans.

"So, he wants to kill you, Inda, correct?" She nodded to him. "Duncan, he wants to take you home, or someplace, for Inda's insane sister to take your blood and make herself even stronger?" Eric asked.

"That about sums it up, yes," Duncan replied.

"Angry, is he?" Eric looked at the Elf line again, shaking his head. "Well, we will see how angry he is when I shove my sword up his...."

"Prince Duncan, Eric!" Brandon interrupted as he raced over. "Look!" And pointed to the enemy lines. A single Elf warrior was walking forward, holding his lance upward with a horse's tail tied to the end, so all could see. The hair blew in the breeze, making it easy to see.

"Hold your fire!" Eric turned to address the Dwarf. "Grilrig, tell your people to hold their fire. That is the parley sign. Looks like someone wishes to talk."

Grilrig passed the message along in Dwarf so his men would not have any accidents.

They watched the Elf walk in the deep snow, struggling in many spots and even falling a few times. Every time he stood, he raised the spear high again.

Once the Elf messenger arrived close enough to Eric's line, the Outrider shouted to him, "That is far enough!" The Elf looked at Eric, confused and scared, but kept walking. "I said stop!" The Elf ignored Eric and kept walking until Inda shouted in elvish.

"He cannot speak your language, silly." Inda smiled at him.

She turned back to the young Elf and asked him in her own language, "What does your lord wish from us?"

"My message is not from my Lord Captain; my message is from the Druid that led us to you." The young Elf's voice shook when he spoke, glancing at her nervously.

Inda nodded to the Elf, turning to Eric and the rest to translate. She turned back to the messenger and asked, "What does the Druid wish to say to us?"

"He wishes you to surrender. He promises on the forest god all will go free if the Prince comes to us, as well as you, my lady." The Elf dropped his head.

"Why did you call me lady?" She smiled before continuing, "Do you not know who I am? Did the Druid tell you my name?"

He dropped his head again and said as though he was shamed, "No, lady, we do not know who you are, only that Prince Duncan is in your care and at all costs, he must come with us alive, and you as well which makes you important." He looked at her and repeated, "At all costs, my lady."

"I am Inda, and I am sure you know who my father is."

The young Elf staggered back in shock.

"Inda," he whispered, took a knee, lowering his head respectfully to her.

"What's going on?" Eric quietly asked, impatient for an update as he watched the scene play out.

She raised a hand to him to quiet him.

"I do not know your name, but I can see the kindness in your eyes." She paused as a tear rolled down his cheek. "You know why I left to the light and found the converts, don't you?"

The Elf nodded and wiped away his tears. "Do you know why my sister wants Prince Duncan?" He looked at the humans, not knowing which one of them was the Prince.

"No."

She smiled again. "So, she will have unlimited magic. Lirdjss will control all of Wreten for my father, and nothing can stop her."

He stared at her. She could see the fear in his eyes as he thought with that type of power what evil her sister, Lirdjss, would do not only to the humans but also to the Elf people.

A second passed when he said with some panic in his voice, "You must not hand him over! I will help you. I have friends that may help!"

Inda let out a breath, and her shoulders relaxed. She waved for him to stand. "Return to your leader and tell them we wish to speak in the center of the clearing."

"Okay." He nodded, though clearly confused.

"Go to your friends and ask them to join us when the fighting starts and to tie something cloth on their arm no matter the color, so we will know who is a friend and who is a foe," Inda said.

The young Elf stood proudly and walked back to his lines. Inda explained everything, but Eric was not sold on her plan.

"So, my lady," Eric's voice dripped sarcasm. "How do you know he is going to do what he said?"

"Did you not see his eyes?" she blurted. Eric shrugged his shoulders.

She rolled her eyes. "Some Elves can see the soul through a person's eyes. He had kind eyes, a kind soul. The man is low-born Eric, forced into this life. He probably wishes he could be at home growing a crop of corn."

Eric shrugged. She shook her head.

"Please, Eric, trust me! My name is known throughout Aethel."

Eric stepped closer and took hold of her shoulders. "I trust you. With my life, I trust you."

5

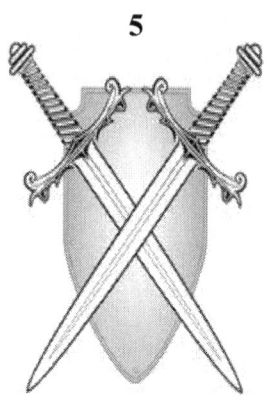

Eric stood watching the Elf position closely. He was waiting for the inevitable Elf charge. Duncan was sitting on his horse, staring intensely, unable to hide his anger. Eric could hear Inda as she stood beside Duncan's horse with her hand on his leg, pleading with him to go inside himself and find his light and bring calm upon him.

Eric returned his gaze back to the Elf lines just in time to see a dozen of the enemy walk to the middle of the field. The middle one carried the spear with the horses' tail, showing their intention was peaceful. Eric could see some wore the armor of officers, while some wore the elite soldier's armor that set them apart from their regular soldiers with gold tree branches that seemed to grow down from their shoulders.

Eric, Inda, Duncan, Davy, and Grilrig took seven Dwarven warriors for protection. The rules of parley clearly dictated only twelve people from either side could be present at the talks.

"Be bloody careful now. You know you cannot trust this type!" Samuel called.

"I am more worried you may eat all my dried meat before I get back." Eric laughed in response.

Samuel chuckled, picked up a bow and tested the drawstring, and turned to Elf and Dwarf warriors around him. "Keep an eye out and be ready. If anything happens, start shooting and hit the ones with the gold on their shoulders first."

Eric kept his hand on his sword hilt as he and the others moved closer to the twelve Elves who had already made it to the center of the clearing. As they approached their enemy, they made out the faces of those who waited for them. Eric looked at the elvish armor as they approached and recognized one style.

Davy observed it was a unique style that they had seen some months back when they were attacked in the cloaking mist.

"Eric," Davy said quietly,

"Yeah," Eric answered the Corporal,

"Look to the left of the Druid." Davy nodded to his left.

Eric found the Druid with the golden thorns that wrapped his upper arms down to his elbows, moved to the left at the Elf standing beside him. This Elf wore the same special armor, with golden thorns on the shoulders, but these pointed upwards.

"Yes, I see them." Eric remembered them well. On the night of the battle in the cloaking mist, he fought two of them that night, one he killed quickly, and the other got away after Eric had relieved the Elf of one of his ears in the fight.

"Look closer," Davy pressed.

Eric did what his friend asked and looked closely at the elite guards. He examined every one of them and saw nothing special about them until he looked into their eyes. In particular, the one standing closest to the Druid was looking at Eric with hatred. Eric stared back at him, realizing this Elf was missing an ear.

"No way!" Eric blurted out, and Davy tried unsuccessfully to stop himself from laughing. He brought his hand up to cover his mouth. Eric was dumbfounded, whispering, "Looks like talking will be a waste of time."

Duncan spoke up. "We have to hear what they say. Custom demands it. They have shown the tail."

They continued forward until they came within ten paces of their enemy. The guards took up a semi-circular position around their own people, remaining silent and still. Eric looked at his old earless friend and politely nodded. The Elf did not acknowledge him beyond his constant glare. Many of the Elves looked at Inda like she was the root of all evil in the world. Eric could see she was uncomfortable, but did an excellent job of not letting it show.

He looked past the party in the center of the Elf line, which seemed to have broken up. Groups had formed and were talking amongst themselves. He watched as some ran from group to group. He looked back at his own lines, which were in perfect formation. Elves, humans, and Dwarves.

Eric turned back to the ones standing in front of him and noticed one was dressed more like the regular Elf soldiers, except for a golden crest on his chest of a horse. Eric had seen these before. He was not part of the elite Elf class, but a simple unit commander, one who had worked his way up the chain after years at the front. Eric directed a simple nod to him, as he was the only one of them he had any respect for. With his long blonde hair under his open-face rounded brass helmet, the older Elf politely nodded back.

"Well, you wish to speak. Let us hear your demands." Prince Duncan broke the silence.

It was the Druid who spoke for the Elf party. His eyes took on a red glow, and his voice was deeper than most Elf males. Most were soft; his was like Eric's uncle Samuel's deep and commanding.

"You are Prince Duncan of Stalwart." The Druid said in a tongue that they all could understand. Duncan felt a chill run under his skin. The Druid turned to Inda, "You, Princess Inda, I will take you home to your father."

Eric looked at her and saw the fear on her face show. She dropped her eyes to the snow below her feet. The Druid looked her up and down, examining the leather armor she was wearing.

"Human leather armor! You are a Princess of Aethel. You dishonor your people," the Druid spat.

"No!" she replied uncomfortably, but she brought her eyes up to his. "I do not!"

The Druid's glowing eyes brightened, shining even in the sunlight as they reflected off the snow. He clenched his teeth and spoke through them. "Princess Inda and Prince Duncan will come with us. The rest of you can leave unharmed!"

Both Davy and Eric laughed.

"I do not think so, mate!" Eric replied as Davy kicked up a foot full of snow at the Druid.

"We have you trapped human, trapped like rats!" the Druid said with an arrogant smile. "Our numbers give us a powerful advantage, plus I sent for more troops. Can you say the same?"

Eric shrugged. "You have me there. Yes, we are trapped. Yes, your numbers are greater than mine, but I will bet one of mine can take ten of yours anytime."

The Elf commander smiled at Eric. Not that he believed him, but it was more like he enjoyed watching someone stand up to the Druid. Inda noticed it as well and looked kindly at him. The two locked eyes for a moment. The commander rolling his head to one side ever so slightly. Eric watched, wondering if the two were communicating in some Elfish way.

"I will give you one chance to turn over the Royals," The Druid demanded, becoming impatient. "Or hostilities will commence. My powers have increased since the last time we met Prince Duncan."

"What a coincidence." Duncan chuckled. "So have mine!"

"Your royal line acts so bravely, but I was there when Simon died." The Druid smiled. "I drank his blood. I will drink yours as well."

Duncan said nothing. He turned around with a look of disgust for the Druid and began walking back to his line. Davy followed the Prince, but not until he gave the Druid a stern look, one finger pointing at his chest.

"See you on the battlefield!"

"You are so full of anger you know nothing else. You do not know love. Is it so foreign to you?" Inda asked the Druid, her head tipping to one side.

His eyes appeared to glow even stronger as she turned and walked away. Those who remained all stood looking at each other in silence for a moment.

"And you? Do you have something to say?" Eric asked, looking at the earless Elf.

The Elf said nothing, only continued his glare.

Eric raised his voice. "Oh, I am sorry, you probably don't hear so well anymore." He laughed again before placing both hands around his mouth, shouting, "I said, do you have anything you would like to say?"

The one-eared Elf instantly threw his shield and spear to the ground and rushed Eric. He pulled his sword out as he advanced. Eric was ready for this, pulled his own, stepped to his right quickly, and blocked a wild blow. Grilrig and the rest of the guard readied weapons. The Elf guards did the same. It was about to kick off into a whole fight when the Elf commander ordered his side to stand down. He turned to Grilrig. "This is single combat only!"

"Agreed!" Grilrig nodded, and both turned their attention to the fight. The Dwarf soldiers at the line cheered loudly as the battle ensued, while the friendly Elves stood silently and watched.

"Get him, Eric, use your speed now!" Samuel yelled from the line.

"Come on, Eric!" Brandon cheered, running forward for a better view.

Davy forced Duncan and Inda to run back to the line for safety. He noticed a look of horror on Inda's face, and more than once, she tried to turn and run back to Eric as he pushed her along.

"Don't worry, Inda. Eric will deal with him easily enough."

The two used their swords with the skill most had never seen before. The Elf was angry and swinging hard with every attack. Eric would step and parry, then step away again, although the deep snow made it difficult. The elite guardsman swung down at Eric's head. While the outrider knocked his blade to his right, the Elf had swung so hard the blade sunk deep into the snow. Before he could react, Eric punched him hard in the neck below his helmet, then thrust his right knee forward, striking him in the ribs. He heard the Elf's air leave his lungs before he dropped to the ground on his left knee. Eric quickly brought his sword up and tried to bring it down on the Elf's torso, but the Elf's superior athletics allowed him to dive forward, rolling to his feet.

The Elf charged at Eric and jumped into the air. He had seen this Elf tactic before. They jumped into the air, turning upside down and either striking their opponent's head or landing on the ground behind them to strike at their back. Eric ducked, dropping to his knees and pivoting. He brought his sword up just as the guardsmen swung at him. Eric beat him into position and blocked the blow. He countered with a strike and hit the Elf's left knee as soon as his feet touched the frozen ground.

The elite guardsman fell to the ground with his leg half cut off, and Eric dove on top of him, driving the hilt of his sword into the chin of the Elf, knocking him unconscious. Eric looked down at the Elf, looking at the one ear sticking out of the helmet's ear hole. He reached down and pulled off the helmet, tossing it at the feel of the Druid, who shook with anger.

"Tell me, Druid, was this man with you when you drank Prince Simon's blood?" The Druid said nothing, turning away to walk back to his lines. Eric stood up and looked at the Commander.

"I have been told you come from honorable people, but this one has none!" Eric drove his sword deep into the throat of the guard. He pulled it out, and without saying another word, stalked back to his lines.

Grilrig laughed, following Eric. The Dwarves scrutinized the Elf lines as they made their way back.

Brandon ran out to meet Eric. He had a smile from ear to ear.

"That was the best thing I have ever seen!" The boy ran into Eric's arms, hugging him like a brother. Samuel waited for Eric with a grin as he made his way up to him, greeting him with a laugh.

"I am going to assume when a parley ends with a sword fight, the negotiations failed."

"Yep, that was the Elf. I took his ear back home in the mist," Eric replied, still panting from the fight.

"Really, small world." Samuel chuckled. "I am not sure why I am laughing. This is going to be a terrible fight with their numbers over there."

"I am not sure of that," Inda said. As they all turned to her, she pointed at the Elf position. There was clearly some arguing happening, and some Elves were pushing others. It appeared like sides were forming. Eric watched closely and noticed the Druid was protectively surrounded by the elite guardsmen. The commander standing between the two groups. The group that had the Druid was considerably smaller than the other and was clearly not the aggressor.

"Well, well." Eric smiled. "Looks like there is trouble brewing."

Davy walked over. "I would guess they don't want to advance on us in this snow. It would be suicide."

"When did you ever see an Elf army not advance when the odds were against them? No buddy, they always do what they are told. Something else is going on."

"There is a revolt happening in their ranks," Inda whispered.

"How do you know?" Eric asked.

"The commander told me during the parley." She grinned.

"But you said nothing to each other. I was right beside you," Davy argued.

"Were you using your mind to speak with him?" Eric remembered the two looking at one another.

Inda nodded. "Not all Elves can do so, but he is able."

"Can we trust him?"

"Evidently, you can." She pointed across the way.

6

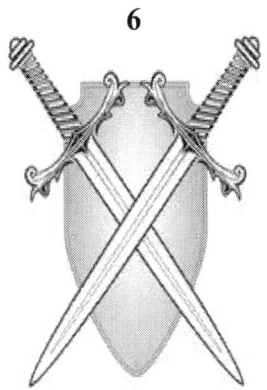

Eric and his friends watched from their position for some time. Evening was setting in, and the darkness was moving in around them. Eric watched in the dimming light while he chewed on dried beef and drank icy water from his waterskin.

The contingent of Elf cavalry that was standing with the Druid was shrinking. As the Elves defected to their commander, many warriors kept their bows trained on the Druid, ready for any unwanted magic he may make.

"Are these guys going to get to fighting, or are they going to talk till dawn? It is getting bloody cold up here!" Samuel impatiently blurted.

Duncan watched closely. Not once since they had returned from the parley had he taken his eyes off the Druid.

"I heard him say he drank Simon's blood," Eric spoke softly, placing his arm over Duncan's shoulder.

"He did. I need to kill him, Eric. I need it as bad as I need to breathe." Duncan sighed, raising his face to the sky.

"I bet. But these Druids are strong, Duncan. It may not be easy. Remember the last time we ran into him."

"I am strong too!" Duncan snapped. "I am not that sick boy anymore, and he killed my brother!"

"I know." Eric watched as a single tear trailed down Duncan's face. Without another word, he handed Duncan a piece of the dried beef.

"Will you help me kill him," Duncan asked around a mouthful of meat.

Eric raised an eyebrow.

"Eric, I want you to help me kill all the Druids that murdered Simon."

"I cannot believe you felt the need to ask." Eric smiled and tore off another bite of the beef.

Suddenly, while they watched the Elf position, a giant fireball built and left the Druid's hand. It struck the Elf commander, causing him to burst into flames. They watched from across the field as he lit another flame and placed a protective shield around himself. His guards and the few followers he had left began fighting with the rest of the Elves, which were well over ten times their number.

Duncan burst away from Eric and ran at the Elf line.

"Duncan, no!" Eric shouted, but the Prince did not listen. He only dropped his cloak, so he could run harder. Eric took flight after him, Davy and Brandon on his heels.

As they ran closer, they could see the Druid flinging fireballs at the rogue Elves. He also used the wind to stir up snow into their faces, preventing them from a direct attack. Eric could hear him laughing. He watched as the Druid spread his arms wide and built a giant fireball ten feet above himself. The friendly Elves began spreading out, but to Eric's surprise, none ran. The Druid pulled his arms down, and the massive fireball flew towards the friendly Elves.

Duncan reached out, and it was like an invisible hand caught the fireball in midair, stopping it. The enraged Prince forced the fireball over the cliff and away.

Duncan slowed, raising his hands. Snow circled around the Druid, blurring the dark Elf's vision. The Dwarves moved forward, firing into the blowing snow with their crossbows.

Duncan looked to the far right, where a large boulder was sticking out of the snow. He reached for it with his power. The boulder lifted out of the frozen ground with a large crack. Eric felt the ground shake just before the Prince threw it into the blowing snow. The ground shook once more as it landed. The Dwarves continued firing as the snow returned to the ground. Many of the dark Elves were dead, but the Druid and most of his men were still very much alive.

The Druid yelled something Elvish at Duncan, his eyes glowing in the dim light, and began walking toward the prince.

Duncan's eyes glowed green as he took several steps towards the Druid. He removed his gloves and tossed them on the ground. Everyone watched the event closely. Inda came running up to stand beside Eric and Davy.

"Stop this!" she screeched.

"Don't let her near Eric," Davy said as he watched, unsure if he should help Duncan or not.

Duncan waited until the Druid made his move, sending a large stream of red energy from his hands toward him. He quickly placed a green light field out in front of himself, blocking the Druid's attack, and held it until the Druid's energy stream dissipated.

Duncan, feeling even bolder, began walking closer as the Druid began sending fireballs and bolts that were not unlike the Paladins at the Prince, which were easily blocked or deflected, some even with his bare hands.

Once Duncan got himself close enough, he sent a brilliant light up into the darkening sky. As the Druid watched it go up, Duncan quickly reached into a small pouch on his belt and pulled out two tiny acorns, palming one in each hand. The Prince's eyes began glowing as he stretched both his arms out to his sides and shouted something in one of the old tongues. Eric watched in amazement as two long green vines grew out of his hands.

Duncan's eyes glowed brighter green, and the two vines glowed as his eyes. The Druid took a nervous step back as he took on a look of confusion at what the Prince was doing just as he began flailing them around casually, as though they were whips.

The Druid stepped back in fear, finally acknowledging that Duncan was much more potent than the last time they met. Duncan lashed the mystical whip forward, striking the Druid in the arm, knocking him backward. The Druid fell to the ground with a cry of pain. His fine-scale armor did nothing to protect him as he looked at the large gash burned into his arm and left a glowing green substance on his wound that continued to burn like acid. Instead of a regular snap of a normal whip sounds, this one gave a loud hiss as though someone had dropped a red-hot horseshoe in a bucket of water.

The Druid raised his hands to try a spell when Duncan hit him again, this time burning a long gash into his chest. The Druid cried out in pain again as he struggled to escape. Duncan let him get several steps before sending the whip around a foot, pulling him to the ground.

The Druid cried out once again began begging for his life. Duncan let him go as he walked closer and stood over him. The whips hissed as they touched the ground. Eric and Davy walked up, watching the remaining Elves, before looking down upon the Druid.

Davy leaned over and whispered into Duncan's ear, "He is much too dangerous to keep alive, Duncan, you know this."

Duncan did nothing as he stood looking at the Druid. Hatred filled the Prince's face as he stared down at the helpless Druid, who was much too terrified to try anything. Duncan raised his hands, and the vine whips retracted into acorns, to which he placed back into the leather pouch on his belt.

Duncan reached to his side and pulled out his sword. He raised it high with the point down, gripped it tightly with both hands, and plunged it downward, hard. The fine Elf armor gave way to the blade as it sunk deep into his chest. The Druid made no sound. He merely reached forward, taking hold of the sword for a moment, just as his head fell back into the snow as he died.

Silence filled the air. Not a sound was heard over the gentle breeze. Eric rounded on the surviving Elves, who stood in shock silently, watching.

"Well, what are we going to do with these guys? There has to be six hundred at least." Eric looked at Inda in question.

Inda stepped out in front of everyone and stopped. The young messenger, who she had spoken with earlier, was the first to come forward. He walked up slowly and knelt in front of her, laying his sword on the ground at her feet. He dropped his face to the snow.

Once he raised it, he said something in Elvish Eric did not understand. Suddenly, the rest of the Elves began moving closer and doing the same.

Brandon walked over. "What are they doing?" he asked, watching cautiously as he approached them.

"They are pleading themselves to me and our cause."

Brandon looked surprised.

Inda simply smiled. "I told you, Brandon, we Elves are not evil people, the Druids who lead us are."

7

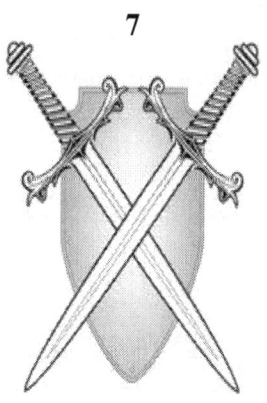

The remaining trip to Stalwart was uneventful until they arrived at the border with close to eight hundred mounted Elves. More than half were still dressed in the Elvish dragon scale armor after volunteering to follow Inda after the Druid was killed.

They were met outside of the border town by close to three thousand well-armed Dwarves and human soldiers. A few hundred civilians had picked up weapons and were ready to fight.

Prince Duncan, along with Grilrig, rode forward to parley and to convince them the Elves with them were, in fact, allies. Even with Prince Duncan's presence, they were given a special escort of a thousand Stalwartian cavalry the rest of the way to Warriors Point. The Dwarf cavalry, who were ordered to take them to the border and return home, stayed with the prince and his ever-growing unit for their protection. It was noticed, but not unexpected, as they entered the human lands; many looked at the Elves with hatred and distrust.

They kept the Dwarf cavalry contingent to separate the Elves and human troops. Prince Duncan wrote a letter to Berar and explained why he commandeered his warriors, and one rider carried it back to Durgh.

It was early evening by the time they had arrived, miles outside of Warriors Point. Most of Eric and Duncan's mixed unit had set up camp in a small wooded valley, out of sight.

The King had received word of his son's intentions and sent more mounted men to escort them back and keep the Elf contingent from falling into trouble or starting any.

Duncan was met by Lord General Bromley Claiborne, who was surrounded by a dozen Outriders and light Calvary. As Prince Duncan road out of the valley, he saw the old General atop his horse waiting for him. Duncan reined his mount toward Claiborne followed by Inda, Samuel, Eric, Brandon, and Davy, as always, were beside the Prince.

As they rode closer, Claiborne looked on at the filthy group coming closer. Duncan noticed he was studying their faces closely. They have all dressed alike in leather armor. Most had weeks of facial hair on their faces.

"He does not know which one of us is, Duncan." Eric chuckled. To which most snickered in the group.

"I want to be Duncan today!" Brandon teased. Which made everyone laugh harder.

They casually made their way to Lord Claiborne and stopped in front of him.

"Where in the name of the brothers is Prince Duncan? I was told he would meet me here!" The General glared as if them standing in front of him was a challenge of sorts.

A slight snicker went over the group as Duncan dismounted from his horse and walked closer, pulling off his leather helmet, allowing his dirty, sweat-soaked hair to fall down. Claiborne looked down at who he thought was another simple Elf hunter. For a moment, Claiborne felt as if he was looking at Prince Simon. His confusion faded as he realized he was expecting to see the same skinny Prince he had watched grow his entire life at the palace in Cardin, not the healthy, well-muscled young man who stood in front of him now.

"Duncan?" Claiborne asked quietly, still unsure of his eyes.

"Uncle Bromley." Duncan smiled at him. This was how Duncan had known him throughout his life. Claiborne climbed down off his horse and walked over and embraced the Prince.

"Your father has been worried sick about you, boy, and so have I."

"Well, no worries, I am back now."

Claiborne stepped back and took a long look at Duncan and his new athletic body. "Well, you certainly look better. I thought you were Simon at first sight."

Duncan smiled, and the two embraced again. After a moment, the prince took the time to introduce all the members of the party. Claiborne took a moment and looked suspiciously over Inda after she pulled her cloak hood down, and he saw her pointed Elf ears. Duncan assured him she was friendly and would make sense once they explained it all to the King.

"Speaking of which, I have orders to take you to the King this instant. He wants you safe behind the city walls," Claiborne said.

There was no argument, and all mounted up and headed east to Warrior's point. The closer they got, the more activity they saw. Once they were a mile from the walls, they could see thousands of tents lined up in straight lines with military proficiency. Soldiers and veterans from all kingdoms had arrived. The King's call for the veterans to return to service had been answered. Eric looked at the thousands of tattooed faces of all ages, walking around the tents, drilling with their weapons, or conversing near the fires. Eric noticed as he rode pasted a row of tents many of the men were old. Their grey hair and wrinkled faces told him they were much too old to be going into battle.

"A lot of grey hair."

Duncan nodded. "I noticed as well."

Lord Claiborne narrowed his eyes. "King William put out the call for all able-bodied veterans to gather at Warrior's Point. Close to fifty thousand have arrived." Without bothering to hide his annoyance, he continued, "Grey hair does not kill a man's pride or his heart." He pulled on his reins, stopping his horse. "He said able-bodied." Claiborne pointed at the men going about their business. "You tell these men who have served honorably they are too old to do it again!"

Eric nodded.

"There is plenty of work an army needs to be done other than swinging a sword. We have arranged these elderly men into units according to their skills and ages and found a job for them. They will guard the supply wagons, scavenge for food, and build fortifications. They understand their roles and want to serve at the King's command."

"As do we all, sir." Eric nodded again.

Claiborne straightened his back in his saddle and hollered, "These old war dogs have plenty of fight left in them!" The surrounding men shouted a cheer. Many held up their swords and weapons as they vocalized their pride. Claiborne grinned at them as he spurred his horse. "If this be the last battle of our lives, may we all die with honor!"

The old soldiers cheered again.

"Long live the King!"

They entered the city. It seemed much different from what it had the last time they were here. There were fewer civilians present, and soldiers lined the streets in every direction. In some streets, they could hardly move. It was so packed. Soldiers of all ages overflowed the streets.

"How many men do we have here?" Duncan asked Claiborne.

Claiborne pursed his lips. "Close to seventy thousand, maybe more now, though some are no better than raw recruits. Unfortunately, we've had some serious setbacks, and we don't have the time needed to train the men to the quality we usually have."

Duncan listened intently as Claiborne continued, "We have easily fifty thousand men ready with men we brought up from other posts. The veterans have arrived in shape, which is good except the Elf army we will face has received reinforcements and is now numbering closer to one hundred and thirty thousand."

"Those numbers are not good. We will have to change our tactics."

"Yes, we will. We have been working on that. Those damn Druids are so strong. They are not like the regular Druids we have matched with our Paladins in the past."

"Leave them to me," Duncan replied confidently.

Claiborne looked at Duncan with concern. "I do not think you understand, Duncan. These Druids are strong."

"I understand, Uncle Bromley. All will be made clear once we see my father." The prince smiled.

8

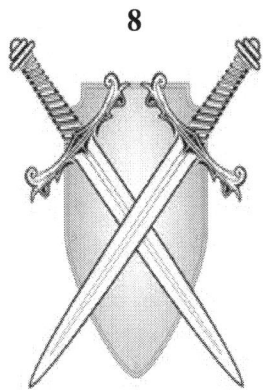

They were led to the city center, to the same estate that belonged to the Lord Commander, where Duncan had stayed when they had picked up Simon's body, which felt like it had been a lifetime ago. There was an overabundance of troops around the walled estate, keeping watch over the king. Duncan looked at the walls for his father's flag. It was dark, but he could hear it flapping in the cool night breeze.

The men at the gate opened it directly when they recognized General Claiborne. They showed him the respect he had earned as he rode through. Once inside, they were quickly met by servants who took their horses from them and asked if they had any immediate needs. Their group followed Duncan and

Claiborne inside two large oak doors to the main residence.

It was an incredibly large three-story stone house that looked more like a castle. They were directed into a large waiting area complete with lavish furniture, usually found in capital cities or royal palaces. Fine wood-crafted shelves held hundreds of books, and paintings of warriors and royals littered the walls. The room was well lit by dozens of candles, and a stone fireplace burned hot.

Brandon bravely walked in and inspected a fine wooden chair with light blue padded cushions, and sat down without thinking of the state of his clothing and armor. Duncan laughed at him for a moment before pointing at his own grubby clothing. Brandon quickly realized what the prince meant and leapt from the chair, almost turning in mid-air to see if he had done any damage. The young squire let out a long sigh when he realized he had not, and moved to a spot in the middle of the room where he was sure he could not do any harm.

They did not have to wait long before the large door to the room swung open with a violent force, and the King himself burst into the room, took five long strides in, stopped and stared at everyone in the room. It did not take the king any time at all to find his son, even with the dramatic changes in his body.

He walked right to him and hugged Duncan tightly; a tear even ran down his cheek, not caring who was watching. Everyone else in the room took a knee, bowed their heads to King William, and waited for him to write them. He let his son go and took a step back to an arm's length while he looked him over.

"This cannot be my son." King William's eyes filled with pride. "My son was a skinny, sick boy. You are a well-muscled warrior." He turned to the rest of the group and gestured for them all to stand. "I am deeply grateful you brought Prince Duncan back to me." He smiled at Duncan again. "Your mother and sister are here in Warriors Point as well. They will be back shortly." The King wrinkled his nose. "You will all be cleaned up and given new clothing before they arrive. It is clear by your smell you have been riding hard. I also told them to make a meal suitable for a returning prince and his warriors."

Duncan nodded. "Father, we must talk now. I have much to tell you."

The King looked at his son and nodded as he understood this was urgent. "Okay, bring who you need and follow me. I will meet the rest of your friends after we talk then."

Duncan motioned for and Eric, Davy, Inda, whose head remained covered in a hood, to follow them. The King pointed to Claiborne to come as well. The rest were released. They left the room in search of hot baths and new clothing.

The King led them down a long hallway and into a room with many maps on a large wooden table. Men in military tunics were working, studying the maps closely. He asked them to give him the room. The soldiers followed his direction without delay.

"What is it, son?" The King asked the moment the door had closed, "I can see you are holding some big news. I'm guessing it has something to do with you using Paladin powers."

"It is much bigger than that, father. I've grown much more powerful than a basic Paladin or the normal Druid we fight daily. I've even killed one of the strong Druids that drank Simon's blood," Duncan said.

"You killed one of the six?" The King asked with pride, his eyes lighting up.

"Yes, I did. I intend on getting the rest of them too."

William nodded and asked, "What about Lirdjss? Can you best her?"

"You know her name?" Duncan asked, surprised.

"Of course, I know her name," King William replied. "Did you not expect me to have spies on their side? I know she is the daughter of the Elf King. I know she has a sister named Inda that went into hiding, and I know she was most likely hiding with the Elves in Dard where you went."

"You know a lot," Duncan said.

King William looked at Eric and the rest and walked over, smoothly pushing past Eric to Davy.

"Good to see you, Corporal Talltree." And before Davy could say anything, King William reached forward and took hold of the hood on Inda's head and gently pulled it back, exposing her face and ears. "Inda, I would be guessing."

"Nice to meet you, your highness," Inda said and politely dropped her head.

William walked over to the table and sat down in one of the chairs, and called for some ale and wine, turned to Eric, noticing his Outrider crest on his cloak.

"I am guessing you are the Outrider that Simon told Duncan to find in the vision?"

"Yes, my lord. Eric Bowman sir, 2nd Seaworth Outriders."

General Claiborne raised an eyebrow, interrupting. "Eric Bowman? Of the 2nd Seaworth Outriders? I have heard of you," Claiborne said, surprised and clearly impressed.

"I've heard of you too, sir, but I never had the pleasure of serving under you."

"You just may yet, son. I am a big fan of the outriders," Claiborne said.

Eric grinned. "It would be my honor, sir."

King William leaned back in his chair, placed one boot up on the table, and stared at the Prince with exaggerated patience.

"Let us start from when you were attacked when you left Warriors Point with Simon's body, shall we? I want every detail, then maybe you can answer the question I asked you. Can you best Lirdjss on the battlefield?"

9

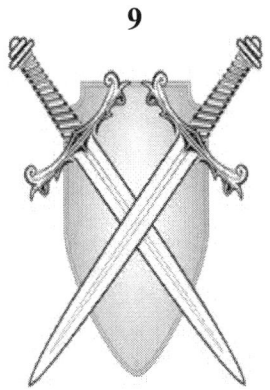

Along with Samuel, Davy, and Brandon, Eric had spent the night in the large estate, in feather beds with soft pillows, and had a long hot bath in the estate's bathhouse. The next morning, still dressed in borrowed servants' clothing, they came down for breakfast.

"No one dressed like this shall meet the queen!" King William said.

Everyone looked at their attire and felt some shame.

"So, we shall take care of that today." After eating breakfast, the King handed Eric a sealed letter and directions to a quartermaster for a new set of kits.

They followed the directions given to them and found the large outfitting station. After showing the duty officer outside the king's letter, were walked to the front of the line, there were hundreds of men waiting in a long line for their turn for a fitting, but a letter barring the royal seal from the King himself gave them precedence over the rest.

An old quartermaster led them away to another building just down the street. He was dressed in a fine light blue tunic that was trimmed in white. He wore no armor. His long grey and rough beard and the three crowns under his eye told them he was a veteran that answered the King's call. He was much too old for combat, nevertheless; he answered the call. They found a job for him, and he seemed content to do his duty in whatever capacity they had chosen for him.

The building he led them to seemed much more refined than the warehouse they had reported to. This one seemed more like living quarters for a Lord with an iron fence wrapped around it. Tied out front. Several horses were in the best condition, with the finest saddles and tac one could buy.

Once they were led inside, the old quartermaster bid them a good day and left them to return to his duties. Eric looked at the building they had just entered. It was not a regular army armor issuing center. Still, an excellent armor merchant, a shop none of them could ever afford, save Grilrig, who already had the best armor money could buy.

The merchant saw them walk in, took one look at the clothing they were wearing, and shook his head. There were two finely dressed men being measured for a suit of plate, looking at them as though they had no business being in the shop. One of which was a fat man who had one crown under his eye. He looked at Eric in his servant's tunic with a wrinkled nose.

"This is not a place for poor peasants. You have no right to be in here!" His remark drew everyone's attention. He gave them a condescending smile. "Even if you could afford the armor, they do not sell to rustic scum. The rest of us wish not to be around you! So, leave before the smell of pig dung gets onto my skin!"

Eric and the rest of them knew immediately this man had some sort of noble birth. His attitude, along with his fat belly and finely cut black hair, told them that. His expensive clothing and jewel-embedded sword hilt tied it all together. Eric knew immediately this man was not someone they could ever challenge.

The armor merchant hurried over to them. He was wearing a red jacket with brown pants and raised his hands as he came closer, shouting.

"His Lordship is right. This is not a place for folk like you. You must leave immediately!" He placed his hand on Eric's chest and gave a solid push. Eric stepped back a few paces, and he felt his body and face go warm with anger. Brandon immediately went to the door and held it open, and waited for his friends.

Eric stood looking the merchant in the eye and heard his uncle's voice. "Come, Eric, we will go back to the quartermaster. He will set us up fine. No need for us to get in any trouble."

Eric handed the armorer the letter with the King's seal. Eric had never read the letter, so he had no idea what it said. The shopkeeper's face went pale when he cracked the king's seal and read the contents. Eric watched as his face went red with embarrassment and turned his attention toward the Lord, who was still standing looking on, offended at their presence with his nose wrinkled. The merchant slowly walked over to the Lord and held the letter up, showing him the King's seal.

"I am sorry, my Lord, they must stay." The fat Lord snapped the letter out of the merchant's hand and examined it. Eric watched as the Lordship's face turned bright red. He looked at Eric in disgust and quickly repositioned himself so his back was to them, and the fitter continued taking his measurements as the armor merchant came back over to them.

"Well, gentlemen, the King's instructions are explicit. You will leave here today with the finest armor I have. I also have instructions to provide you some new clothing, at his highness's expense."

Eric shrugged his shoulders at the merchant, who stepped closer and said quietly after he looked to see if the Lord was listening, "Please, take my apology for asking you to leave. You know these lordish types."

"Oh, I do." Samuel nodded. "Too much gold and no brains."

A snicker went over the room, but the Lord did not say a word.

Eric sat down in a chair, began taking off his boots. "We should have brought Inda with us. She needs some new clothes."

Davy looked at Eric and shook his head. "Keep her out of sight, Eric. There are too many folks here eager to fight the Elves. This is not the place for her."

"Yeah, I guess you're right. Those pretty pointed ears of hers will make her stand out."

"Yes, they would." Davy replied, "Besides, she is much too pretty to be walking the streets with this many soldiers anyway, and you know we would end up having to do some killing in the middle of the streets."

"Yep." Brandon interrupted with a grin, "Her being an Elf or not, she has been so nice to me, I would happily kill anyone who threatened her ladyship."

Suddenly, the fat Lord swung around and shouted, "Did I hear you correctly? Are you peasant scum, a rabble of Elf lovers? Or are you simple traitors?"

"Oh, no, my Lord, I was merely kidding." Brandon quickly stepped back, wishing he never said a word.

The Lord turned and stepped closer in a challenging stance. "Is the King and this army so desperate for men he has handpicked some traitors and Elf lovers to come north with us?" He paused for a moment and grinned. "You are the peasant scum who went north with Prince Duncan, are you?" He let out a laugh and added, "Tell me which one of you is the dog who is bedding the Elf female?"

Eric took a step closer and looked the important man in the eye, and said slowly, "Be careful, your lordship, the next words that leave your mouth will determine the rest of your life."

The Lord laughed and walked to the front door and shouted, "Gilliam, Turmel, all of you come in here!" A second later, three men in mail armor in the King's white and blue colors rushed into the shop. Each had one crown under their eye. "These men were just leaving. Get them out of this establishment immediately! I will not be in the same room as a man who willingly shares his bed with an Elf witch!"

The biggest of the bunch was a tall, thick man with a full beard and an open-face helmet. He stepped forward and said with a commanding voice, "Come on, boys, time to go now. You heard his lordship!"

"I did." While trying to hold his temper, Eric replied, "But, the King himself has granted this armorer the command to provide my friends and me new armor, and I will not leave until we have it all."

Davy laughed and stepped up beside Eric. "Now, boys, you need to think long and hard about how far you are willing to take this. Like my friend said, it is the King's command."

His lordship shouted from behind the men, "King's command or not, they will leave and come back after I am done. I will not be in the same room as Elf-loving peasant scum."

There was silence for a moment as the shopkeeper ran out of the building into the street, shouting, "Peacekeeper! I need a Peacekeeper now!" When the door closed behind him, a second guard with many missing teeth and a large pustule on his nose stepped closer. "Is that true, boys? Are you a bunch of Elf lovers? Do you know what I did to Elf lovers when I was at Rockworth?"

Eric looked at his chest and saw an Outrider's crest, and the anger increased with this man's disrespect.

"Oh, please," Samuel replied loudly as he pulled out his sword and rested it on his shoulder. "Please fill us in."

The filthy man smiled and placed his hand on his sword hilt. "Well, it is like this! Elf women are to be taken by force. I've had a dozen of them when we raided their towns and villages." His smile grew bigger. "But any man who willingly takes one into his bed and forms any type of intimate relationship with is a complete traitor to his race, and I would be happy to be the one to deal with them accordingly." The toothless man dragged out his sword and grinned as he set the tip on the floor between his toes.

Eric shook his head and pulled his own sword from his scabbard, and thundered, "And when, may I ask, will you perform this horrible act on me? I am not very busy at this moment!"

The toothless guard lifted his weapon, as did Eric. The tips of their blades touched, and Davy yelled,

"Oh, yeah! Here we go!" He took post beside Eric, and Samuel did the same on the other side, and Brandon shouted as he pulled his own weapon.

"You guys are going to get it, and you asked for it!"

The door suddenly burst open, and the shopkeeper ran inside. He was followed by a Peacekeeper with a large moustache and three crowns under his eye. Eric recognized him immediately as Corporal Rudderham of the King's Peacekeepers. Some time ago, Eric had supported the Corporal in a fight against a band of ruffians in the town of Greenbank on his way north after his discharge from the army.

"What's going on here!" Rudderham shouted heavily with annoyance. A smile crept over the Peacekeeper's face as he saw Eric. "Bowman?"

"Corporal Rudderham," Eric replied fondly, making known he remembered him.

"Why is this shopkeeper so annoyed, and why, in the name of the brothers, is everyone armed like they are going to shed blood in this fine establishment and ruin the carpet," Rudderham said.

"These dogs will not leave! Corporal, I demand you remove them at once!" The Lord shouted.

Rudderham looked at the Lord and his three men standing opposite Eric and his party in silence. He turned away from the Lord. "Eric, what happened?"

Eric said nothing. He simply handed him the letter meant for the armorer. The Peacekeeper read the letter over, examined the King's seal, smiled, handed the letter back to Eric, turned to the Lord, and asked,

"Why do you demand these men leave the facility, Lord... What is your name Sir?"

The man announced proudly, "I am Lord Gransel of Melton."

"Melton?" Rudderham replied, wondering where it was.

Gransel had the look of victory on his face and spoke with authority, "Yes, Melton, it is south of...."

"Queens Port!" Eric interrupted. "It is a small village a half day's ride south of Queens Port. There may be a hundred folk there at the most."

"Ahh." Rudderham acknowledged Eric and turned to Lord Gransel. "Why do you wish them to leave the shop, good Sir?"

"I do not need to explain myself to a common Peacekeeper. I am a Lord, and you are not! Just make them leave, or I will have you flogged!"

Gransel's toothless guard stepped in front of Rudderham and boasted, "He's serious peacekeeper. Maybe I'll use the whip myself on your back."

Rudderham smiled, took a step back, and raised his voice. "There is a slight problem here. We have a man with a fancy title and three men at arms. We also have a party of common men with a letter from the King allowing them to receive armor from this merchant at his highness's expense."

"I see not a problem." The toothless man gloated. "They can come back later when my Lord is done and not one minute before."

Rudderham looked the toothless man in the eye. "Why am I not surprised you do not see a problem?" The experienced peacekeeper threw a hard-right black leather gloved hand and struck the toothless man in the jaw, causing him to fall to the floor unconscious.

The large man thrust his sword at Rudderham's chest, but he stepped to his left, knocked the blade away with his right hand, and kicked the big man in the knee, causing him to fall.

The third man at arms was already going down after Samuel used the flat of his sword blade across the side of his head, sending him into the same state as his toothless friend.

The big man tried standing, but Davy stepped in and kicked him in the face, stepped even closer and punched him directly in the mouth. The man fell backward to the floor, unmoving.

Lord Gransel protested immediately. "I will make sure the Lord Commander of Warriors Point hears of this! You will all be…" Gransel's tirade was cut short when Rudderham punched him in the throat. Gransel fell to the floor, looking for his wind. Rudderham followed up the attack with a swift kick to his stomach, ensuring he was staying down and quiet.

The enraged Peacekeeper circled the gasping Lord and shouted, "You don't know when to shut your mouth, do you?"

Eric smiled as he watched Rudderham.

"This man is carrying a letter from the King! This means he gets priority over anyone else, even you! Well, especially you, even though you have a lofty title and rule over six folks and twelve goats!" He paused and looked at Eric and his friends, and gave a small wink. "I have travelled a long way and just got to town, and I need some food and a bed. I am in no mood for this nonsense. So, pick up your men and get them out of here, my Lord, and I will convince my old friend here not to tell the King of your disrespect to these men he clearly holds in high regard."

The men were assisted to the door and tossed out onto the street. Eric and Rudderham embraced briefly like old friends, and Rudderham shouted with laughter in his voice, "Wow, I've seen you twice, Outrider, and both times we have taken on weak men with armed guards."

"That is the way of the brothers," Eric replied. "You travelled up here for the fun, I see."

Rudderham nodded. "I am the King's man and always will be, but listen, since you have a letter from the King, is there any way you could you speak to him about the incident in here? His Lordship may be upset about the punch to his throat and try to get even."

"I am staying at the Lord Commander's estate with the King. I will make sure of it." Eric laughed.

Rudderham's eyes went wide. "The Lord Commander's Estate? What's happened since I last saw you?"

The two spent some time talking while Eric was fitted with his armor. Eric filled the peacekeeper in with every detail of his adventure to the north and back. Rudderham sat listening and shaking his head at the tale, laughing frequently, and asked questions as he listened.

"Vandians and Trolls?" he asked. "Amazing you survived it all."

Eric turned to the mirror, admiring his new armor. "A few times, I wondered myself."

The peacekeeper stood, placing a hand on Eric's shoulder. "Well, Eric, I must be moving on. I need to find my posting and report myself in. I wish we could talk longer, but I am off."

They said their goodbyes and the proud Peacekeeper headed for the door. "We will drink a tavern dry of ale after we win this battle."

10

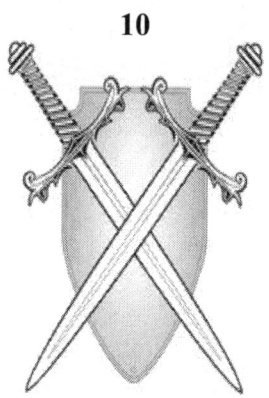

They spent the morning and afternoon getting fitted for the best armor the merchant had. Eric received a set of lightweight Outrider leather and mail, with gloves and the rounded helmet.

Davy received a new set of the heavy plate he so missed, while Samuel received the same. Brandon's order was more like Eric's, lightweight mail and leather with suitable gloves and fine boots, rounded helmet with metal elbow guards, and grieves on his forearms. A man came into the room and dropped off new enchanted weapons for them all. Eric turned the new sword down, as his sword was trusted and loved by him.

Hours had passed by in the shop until they left wearing their new armor, and they walked down the crowded street. Like an Outrider again wearing his uniform, Eric felt good. His crest was shining proudly on his chest. All of them had a little something extra in their step as they made their way back until Eric heard his name being called out in the crowd.

He looked around, seeing nothing but soldiers. He heard it again.

Samuel let out an excited howl, "Well, would you look at that!"

Eric still could not see who called his name until the man was on top of him. His father Nathan was dressed in light cavalry armor, light blue tunic, round helmet, partial plate on the chest. He hugged his son hard the second he got close enough to wrap his arms around him.

"Thank the brothers, you are all alive!" Nathan said as he held his son. Eric was in a state of shock to see his father there in Warrior's Point.

"Why are you in uniform, dad?" Eric suspiciously inquired and thought of the wound to his leg from the battle in the cloaking mist. "Your leg? You were walking with a limp the last time I saw you."

Samuel laughed at Eric just as Nathan reached for his brother and hugged him just as hard as he did his son. Eric wanted an answer to his question.

"Dad, why are you in uniform?"

Nathan faced his son. "I am part of the new 33rd Light Cavalry Brigade in charge of the safe management and delivery of baggage and supplies." He smiled. "My infantry days are done with this bum leg, son, but we Bowmans do our duty, and I can still ride a horse. They put me in with a large unit of good old veterans that are too damn old to be here but refused to stay home."

Eric hugged his dad again. "Where's mom?"

Nathan patted Eric on the shoulder. "She's with your sister at the Wardells."

"With the Wardells?" Eric snapped, "Why did you not send them south to Cardin? It would be much safer there."

"They wouldn't go, you know your mother and sister." Nathan shrugged his shoulders.

"Okay then," Eric replied, wishing there was something else he could say, but he knew his mother like his father said.

Nathan smiled and slapped his son on the back. "They are safe, warm, and have a belly full of pork."

Eric grinned and said with pride, "You won't believe the adventure we have had."

Samuel jumped in, "Brother, you really won't believe it, and we will need a dozen jugs of ale to tell it all."

11

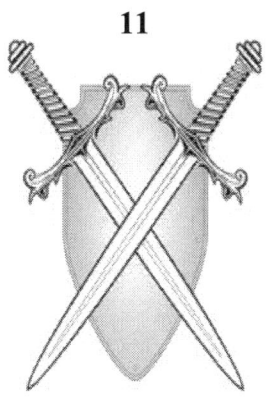

Nathan had followed Eric and the men back to the estate, where they would stay again. They told him much of the tale of their quest on the walk, and Nathan was eager to hear the adventure in full. Once at the estate gates, Nathan was stopped by the King's men and was not allowed inside. Brandon ran in and retrieved Duncan, who quickly came out to see Nathan again. The Prince gratefully granted Nathan access to be with his son and went a step farther and had him placed under his command, so he would serve with his son and brother when they took to the march again in a few days.

The three Bowman men sat up late, drinking ale and answering more of Nathan's questions of the quest north and back again. They were seated at a table in a small library filled with books on strategy and war. Maps and scrolls were piled high on shelving units. The room was lit by oil lamps. Eric kept placing his hand over the flame until it would hurt, then would quickly pull it away, and Samuel would playfully slap at Eric's head every time and say, "See, I told you, dummy." And all would laugh.

"So, Eric?" Nathan asked for the second time. "This moon bowl, it showed you the brothers coming to you and blessing you with great speed and with the skills of a soldier?"

"Yes," Eric replied to his father, knowing how ridiculous it sounded.

Samuel chuckled. "I couldn't believe it either, Nathan, but he's as quick as a cat with that sword. You should've seen him hacking up those Trolls when we first rode into Dard."

Nathan rolled his eyes. "Trolls, now I know you two are pulling my leg." He took a drink of ale and laughed out loud, "Next, you will tell me you think these Elves you brought down with you have truly found the light." He laughed again as he took another drink of the ale.

The grin left Eric's face. "They are, dad. We have learned the Elves are not bad folk. It's the dark Druids that rule them. The Druids take power from the darkness and have basically enslaved their own people."

"Come on, Eric." Nathan replied, not believing a word of it. "After all you have been through, after all this family has done in the war for the past five hundred years, you believe them?"

Eric sat silently, holding back his anger, not wanting to say anything in anger. It was Samuel who then broke the bigger news to Eric's father.

"Well, brother, I best tell you now before we have too much ale."

"No, Samuel!" Eric snapped.

Nathan set his cup down and leaned forward. "No, Samuel, what?" He looked his son in the eyes closely and asked him plainly, just as he would when Eric was a child and had been up to no good. "What is it you are afraid of me finding out, boy?" Samuel let out a quiet snicker and took a drink of his ale.

Eric took a nervous drink. "The Elf that has been teaching Duncan…"

"Yes. The female one, Inda, you said her name was, I believe."

"She is the Elf King's daughter," Eric said while his father followed him. "She is also the sister of the dark Druid that killed Prince Simon."

Nathan laughed. "Exactly my point Eric, you cannot trust these so-called friendly Elves."

Samuel chuckled, "Just wait, brother, it gets better."

Nathan stared at Eric. He let out a long sigh. "If you have a point, just get to it!"

Eric lifted his goblet and took a long drink of his ale, then set the cup down and began the explanation. "The female Elf, her name is Inda, has become special to me."

Nathan looked at his son and replied one word, "Special?" He then looked to his brother, who was smirking and shouted, "And you allowed this!"

"Hey, don't blame me. You raised him to be as pig-headed as you!"

Nathan looked back at Eric. "Special? As you are in love with her?"

Eric nodded.

"And I suppose you think she loves you back then."

"She does," Eric replied quietly, but the tension was building in him and the anger was showing on his face.

Nathan stopped yelling and filled his goblet with ale from the large clay jug that sat on the table in front of him, and calmed himself.

"Look, Eric, we Bowmans, we have killed the Elves by the hundreds over the centuries, by the hundreds, Eric. Does she know this?"

Inda coughed, standing in the open doorway to the library. "I do now."

Eric looked at her with embarrassment all over his face.

"My lady." Samuel gritted his teeth and held up his goblet politely to her. She smiled at Samuel, then turned to Eric.

"Will you introduce me to your father, please?"

Eric stood and walked over to her. Even in the tense moment, her face still captivated him. She was dressed in a delicate white dress. On her shoulders was a light grey scarf that complimented her eyes, making them even more attractive than usual. Her long hair hung loose down to her shoulders, leaving just the tips of her pointed ears ever so slightly poking out.

Eric took her gently by the arm and led her closer to his father, who was now standing, looking red-faced.

"Dad, this is Inda. Inda, this is my father, Nathan Bowman."

Nathan said nothing and leaned over and took her hand in his, then placed his other hand on top of hers and held it for a moment. The two were silent, just looking at each other. Eric watched as she tilted her head ever so slightly to the right and smiled.

Nathan smiled back. "Yes, you are right, my lady." They both laughed. Nathan slowly let her hand go, then sat down as a tear ran down his cheek. He added, "My apologies to you, Inda. I am sorry for speaking ill of you."

Eric was confused about what had just happened. Nathan looked at his son.

"You are correct, Eric. She is special indeed. Be sure to treat her well. Your mother will love her."

Inda reached up and took Eric by the neck, kissing him on the cheek, and whispered in his ear.

"Do not stay up too late, I will be waiting." She then smiled at Samuel, who winked back and left the room.

Eric was still confused and looked at his father for an answer.

"She can speak with her mind Eric, she told me something about myself no one else could ever have known, something from the war." Nathan wiped another tear away, "You treat her right, son."

Eric stared at his father, confused. "What did she say? A moment ago, you were more of a racist than I ever was, and now this?"

12

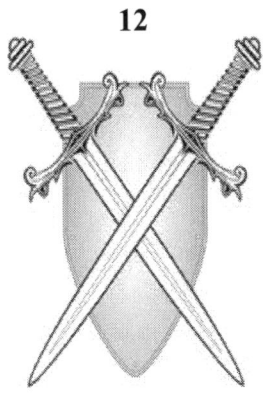

It was still dark in the early morning when Prince Duncan watched Brandon finish tying his bags to the rear of his horse in the crowded courtyard of the estate. Duncan's mother and sister watched closely as he climbed aboard his horse and took the reins in his hands. The sound of thousands of men marching came over the estate's walls as soldiers' boots stamped on the stone-paved streets, combined with the thousands of shoed hooves of horses and the wheel wagons and carts that carried countless tons of supplies and equipment was almost deafening.

Prince Duncan's father was already mounted in full armor and ready to leave, but waited patiently for his wife to say her goodbyes to her son, who she only had a few days with since his arrival at Warriors Point to this moment. Tears ran down the Queen's face as she pulled his arm, forcing her son to lean down and hug his mother. His little sister Princess Ana wept as hard as her mother but stood back watching.

Duncan reached down and stroked his mother's cheek, wiping away the lone tear. "Don't worry, we will be home in a week or two with a glorious victory under our belts."

She swallowed hard and nodded. "I will pray to the brothers to be kind to me and make it so."

Duncan smiled and gently spurred his horse, and moved to his father's side just in time for King William to blow his wife a kiss. She mouthed the words, "I love you," in return.

The King raised his hand and ordered the column to move, and all at once, the large group of mounted knights and soldiers began riding towards the eastern gate of the city. Just as Corporal Talltree exited the estate gate, he heard his name called from the Queen. He looked back as she rushed closer to him, shouting,

"Davy, you keep him safe. Please, Davy, watch over them both."

The loyal bodyguard smiled.

"On my own life, my Queen!" He faced forward where Duncan was looking back at him. Davy grinned. "Don't I always bring you home?"

Eric, Brandon, Samuel, and Nathan were there as well, with Inda, dressed in a fine set of lightweight leather armor that perfectly fit her body. Eric insisted she ride next to him, and the two whispered to each other throughout the ride until Nathan took his place as he wished to get to know the Elf, who he figured may very well end being part of his family someday in the future.

Once miles away from the city, Eric took the time to join up with a group of the Kings' favourite Outriders led by a tall one named Cheese and do a patrol.

They marched hard to the northeast, miles passed under them, and by the time the daylight was leaving, they had already moved well beyond where the road was paved with stone to simple packed earth and all too often mud hole.

Duncan pulled his cloak tighter when he felt the cool air and asked his father, "Where are we camping for the night?"

"We will not be stopping!" The King said. "This is a forced march until we reach the ground I have selected for this battle."

Duncan nodded. "And when will we arrive at the ground you are talking about?"

The King considered this. "If we keep a strong pace like this, maybe mid or late tomorrow night."

"Very well," Duncan replied, then looked forward, thinking of what was coming in the days or weeks. He then said to his father, "Do you expect to run into any Elf patrols before we hit our destination?"

King William shrugged. "I left explicit orders for our Outriders to make sure the word of our march does not get back to the Elf army."

"That may be difficult if they see us first," Duncan replied.

The King smiled. "A few thousand experienced Outriders and light cavalry are in front to clear us a path, don't worry about that, son. They will do their job alright."

Duncan smiled at his father and said sadly, "I wish Simon were here with us. He would have liked the three of us being on the march together."

"Yes, he would have." The King replied as he remembered fondly of his oldest son.

They were cresting a hill when the King and Duncan reined their horses out of the column and off to the side of the road, where they stopped and looked back at the tightly packed and seemingly endless column of men and horses marching. Even in the dimming light, they could see tens of thousands stretched for so many miles back.

The two sat on their mounts, talking as the army marched past them. Many of the men cheered the King and his son when they saw them. William would smile at each of them and sometimes throw a fun verbal joust at them, which always got the surrounding men laughing. One young man shouted to Duncan.

"Prince Duncan, I heard you're a wizard these days. Could his highness conjure us up a wheel of cheese for supper?" The surrounding men laughed, as did Duncan.

"Sorry, lads, I am not hungry just at this minute."

Which caused them all to laugh again as they continued their arduous march. Duncan could hear some of them who had seen him years prior talking of how large he had become, and they seemed proud of their new Crown Prince.

"Well done." William said proudly. "It is always important to show good spirits when heading into battle, especially a major battle like this one." They were interrupted by another voice from the column.

"Well, well." An old soldier shouted, "Prince Duncan is looking mighty sporty these days."

Duncan looked and saw a grey-haired old soldier with three crowns under his eye and clearly had been retired for some time. The old man was walking with a terrible limp that made him wince with every other step.

"Why are you limping, old-timer?" Duncan asked.

The old soldier replied as though he was embarrassed, "I am fine, your Lordship."

Duncan then playfully shouted, "Corns on your feet, I bet." And the men around laughed, the old soldier said nothing, he only smiled and continued marching. As Duncan watched him closer, he could tell the old man was in pain. He dismounted and hurried over, pulling the soldier out of the ranks.

"Hold the column!" King William shouted. His order was relayed down in both directions until the entire army came to a stop, and then he ordered, "We will stop for a small rest to take in food and drink, rest in place!"

This order was relayed as well, and the men began drinking water from their skins and eating what they had carried with them.

Duncan walked the older man off the road and sat him down, and looked at his left ankle.

"Take off your boot, sir," Duncan said.

The old soldier looked at the younger men who watched on and said defensively, "I am fine, my Prince, just a sprain."

"We will see then, won't we," Duncan reached down and pulled off his leather boot, and looked at the ankle of the man. It was swollen but not from a sprain. He had a large gash on the underside of his foot, which had become infected. As Duncan examined it, he could smell the puss that was oozing out and winced.

King William dismounted and looked at the infection. "This wound is many days old. Why did you not report this before we left?"

The old soldier lowered his head to the ground in shame. "Because I would not have been able to come, my King. It would be a great dishonor to my family."

William sighed, "I understand, soldier, but that wound is terribly infected, and unless the Paladins can do something, you will die. I fear the infection has gone too far now."

"I will make the march and do my duty, sir," the old soldier said, "With honor, sir."

King William stood tall and shouted for a Paladin.

"That won't be necessary." Duncan repositioned himself next to the man and pulled off his gloves. He placed his hands on the soldier's ankle and closed his eyes. The soldiers in the line watched as they ate their bread and cheese. They observed as Duncan opened his eyes, which glowed green, his hands shone as well, and the glow covered the man's ankle and foot. Many of the men watching had seen the Paladins heal men before, but it was never like this. None of them had seen the green glow before.

A few moments later, Duncan closed his eyes, and the glow left. The Prince then stood and looked at the old soldier and asked, "How does that feel?"

The old man reached down and felt his foot and gave a hoot of joy and shouted, "Well, that is amazing, alright!" Then jumped to his feet and bounced on it. "You fixed it, your highness." He then reached over and took his wrist and clenched it as he dropped to his knees. "I am loyal to the royal family and always have been." A tear rolled down his face as the old man was wracked with emotion. "Thank you for being loyal to me. I would kiss you if the boys weren't watching."

Duncan laughed at the comment and replied, "Your loyalty to Stalwart is all the thanks I need, good soldier." Duncan watched as the old man placed his boot back and retook his place in line. He could hear men talking about his glowing eyes.

"I have heard he is strong enough to fight the Druid. Maybe we have a chance."

A few moments later, William gave the order to continue the march, and the two stood on the hill, watching for a time. Duncan looked at his father and noticed he was smiling proudly.

"What?" Duncan asked, wondering what he was thinking.

The King grinned.

"I am just proud to see the man you have become."

13

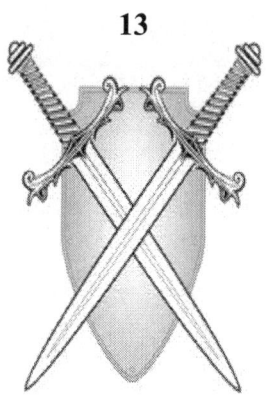

Eric was sitting in the woods, not far off the road. He had been scouting with Cheese and the rest of the Outriders for almost two days, keeping well ahead of the army as it advanced.

King William had given strict orders to illuminate as many of the enemy scouting patrols as possible to prevent them from being able to report their movements back. Cheese had expert knowledge of the forest in the area around Cyrworth and had taken Eric and the other fifty men far ahead of the army to look for any signs of the enemy.

It was late afternoon when they stopped off the road in the trees, waiting for any sign of movement from the North. Eric looked around and felt good about this position, turning his gaze to the tall

Outrider that knew his business. It was clear why the King had grown to trust him so much. Eric had removed his bow from his saddle and strung the string on it as if the enemy had shown up.

Cheese slowly crept down the line of men, making sure all was good. Eric greeted him with a nod just as he sat down beside him and pulled out his water skin.

"Eric," Cheese said quietly. "So, I hear you were on a grand quest with the Prince."

"I was," Eric replied. "We went way up into the north, so Prince Duncan could meet the Elves that had defected to the light."

Cheese nodded and nervously asked, "Do you really think the Prince has powers that can beat the female Druid leading the Elf army?"

"I've seen him in action, Cheese," Eric replied confidently. "He easily took care of an underling to Lirdjss. I watched it happen."

"I hope so," Cheese said. "If we lose this fight, I fear we will lose the war."

"I will never give up fighting. Never!" Eric said.

"Neither will I," Cheese retorted, "But if we lose this one, we'll all be dead, I fear."

"I'll agree with you on that, brother." Eric adjusted himself on the ground, finding a more comfortable position. "At least we will die on our feet. No whip will touch my back."

Cheese grinned. "I will die with my sword coated in Elf blood!" Then he reached to his waist, patted his blade softly. "My hopes are my father will know we died with honor."

"My father is with the army," Eric said.

"Is it true you guys and Prince Duncan brought down like eighteen hundred Elf cavalry and a few hundred Dwarves on the ram?"

Eric chuckled. "It is more like eight hundred and about two hundred Dwarves, and yes, they are going to fight with us." Eric watched as Cheese's face cringed at the thought of fighting side by side with the Elves against other Elves. Then Eric added, "On my word as an Outrider, they are true to us."

Cheese blurted, "I also heard you are in love with that pretty female Elf, and she is a witch, a fortune teller."

Eric grinned and, not finding the right words, changed the subject. "I wonder if the army has made it to the battle site yet."

Cheese looked up through the branches of the trees above him to the position of the sun. "They should be close, maybe a couple of hours away if they could keep the pace they were marching to when we left them."

Eric was about to say something when he heard a familiar bird call that was a signal taught to every Outrider. "Someone is coming!"

He readied his bow and waited, watching the road. He looked to his right and saw four Elf riders coming fast south, spurring their horses hard, keeping them at a full gallop. Cheese placed two figures in his mouth and waited for the signal for the archers to shoot—a few seconds passed when he let out a loud whistle. A dozen men let fly their arrows at the four Elf scouts, and a second after that, they all fell to the ground and rolled until they lay unmoving. Eric and Cheese, with several others, rushed out and drug them into the woods out of sight.

A fast search of their bodies turned up a map of the northern road. Cheese and Eric studied it and found no markings on the position that the army was approaching.

"Well, that's a good sign. Maybe we can surprise them," Eric said.

"I doubt it will be much of a surprise," Cheese said, "They will come in force once none of their scouting patrols return, and we are close to Cyrworth where the main Elf body is stationed."

"Cyrworth. I've always wanted to see it," Eric said.

"Funny. I always wanted to see Seaworth. I would bet it was much better than the winters up here."

Eric chuckled at his brother, Outrider. "Seaworth is great. You can swim in the cool ocean to escape the blistering heat that makes the rock inside the fortress so hot that it almost boils you alive in your armor," Eric joked. "The Outrider long-range patrols into the deep desert where it was impossible to bring enough water, the almost constant state of siege, the massive rocks being thrown at us from catapults, yeah Seaworth was great."

Both men then chuckled and quietly traded stories of their time in the great fortresses until the signal was heard again.

Eric was readying another arrow when another outrider came running. Not being overly careful about making noise, Eric knew something terrible was coming.

The older Outrider, who was running to Cheese, stopped and dropped to his knees. His beard was thick and dark. He had two crowns under his eye and took Cheese by the shoulder and reported.

"They are miles away yet, Cheese, but by the size of it, I think it is the entire Elf army."

Cheese looked at the Outrider across from him. Eric could tell he was experienced and a cool customer. He could also tell, just by the look on Cheese's face, he trusted the man.

Eric wasted no time knowing what the order would be, and they all stood at the same time. He unstrung his bow as he made his way to his horse. As he found his mount, he heard Cheese shout, "Mount up, lads time to run for it! If we get hit on the way back, and I die, ride for yourselves and get to the King. Report the entire enemy army was last seen here at this position!"

As the unit mounted up and formed on the road and started at a gallop on the way south again, Eric's excitement grew.

The battle of our time will happen within a few days.

14

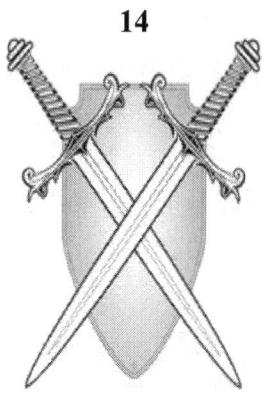

King William stood up top of the hill's highest point and looked northeast down the road it overlooked. He then turned behind him at the endless trail of personnel that had followed him here. He had arrived at the battlefield he had scouted some weeks back, well ahead of this expected time of arrival, and was proud of that. There was much preparation that needed to be done before the battle, and they needed all the time they could get.

The view from up the highest point on the hill went on for many miles. The ground was grass with a few trees they would soon cut down. The slope was steep in many points but not unpassable, and the surrounding area had a circle of hills that would provide them with an excellent natural fortress the Elf

Druids could not knock down with magic. There was enough space in the middle. He could hide most of his forces on the backside of the hill, out of sight from the enemy spell casters.

Prince Duncan road up beside the King. Followed by Brandon, Samuel, Nathan, and Davy, who never left his side.

"This is it Duncan. All my years of studying tactics, all the battles I've fought, and everything I've learned all comes down to this moment in history on this hill," the King said.

Duncan looked around the soon-to-be battlefield and nodded. "It really is a wonderful location, father." The prince let out a sigh of relief. "It very good ground."

The King nodded. "I had seen it years ago when coming back from Cyrworth and always kept it in mind for a fallback location for a day just like this." He then looked at Duncan and pointed to his right at a red flag, "Your Elf and the Dwarven unit, I want them placed there on the right. You will hold them in reserve and stay on the backside of the hill out of sight." Then King William asked, "Who did you put in command of that mixed unit, anyway?"

"I decided just today to put Eric Bowman in charge of that unit. He is out scouting with Cheese and the Outriders right now. I will inform him the moment he gets back."

"Bowman," the King repeated. "He was the Outrider your visions told you to find, correct?"

"Yes, he is young, but he is a good soldier, father. I trust him fully."

"Good. He may be perfect for a job I have in mind for the Elves in that unit of yours. Just make sure you keep them out of sight, that is important, and did they bring their old Elf armor like I said?"

"They did." Eric replied, wondering what his father was thinking. "They are currently wearing the new chain mail we gave them, but they brought it."

"Good, that will be good." The King climbed off his horse and looked north again. The daylight was leaving, and he took a long deep breath in, then let it out slowly. He saw a group of riders galloping hard on the road, coming towards his new position, off in the distance. He smiled once he realized it was Cheese, and judging by the way they were riding, he knew it was bad news. The King whispered, "Ah, here comes Cheese with the bad news I knew he would have for me."

He turned around to yell, "Fetch me, General Claiborne! Tell the unit commanders I want the work on the trench works and palisades to begin immediately! They all know where they are to be placed. I want no excuses!"

Messengers rode off in all directions, carrying the King's word. William returned his attention to Cheese and his men, who had just reached the base of the hill.

Duncan walked over beside him. "Ah, here is Eric Bowman now."

"Make sure he knows where to put his unit and make sure he knows to keep them out of sight. That is important. Keep them out of sight," King William said.

15

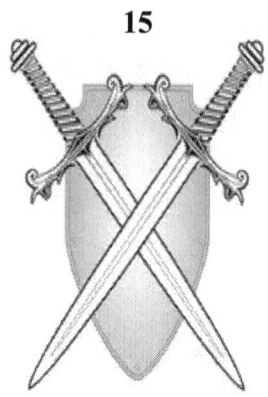

Eric was in a slight state of shock, having just learned of his promotion to a unit commander. He did not expect the King would have placed him in charge of a unit so large so quickly. Ever since he met Prince Duncan, Eric was secretly hoping for a knighthood for a reward. He even dreamed of maybe a minor lordship with his own lands, but knew that was basically impossible being as low born as he was.

He thought of the fighters he would lead and calmed down. He had fought the Elves long enough to know they were solid fighters, and the bump in his pay would be dramatic. As the hours went by, he felt happy about this appointment, but he did not kid himself one bit as he felt some disappointment. Though he did not let it show.

It had been almost two days since he arrived at the King's position high upon the hill, which the men simply and affectionately called William's Hill in honor of the King. Eric walked from the backside up to the top with his father. Nathan still had a limp from the wound he took on the night of the cloaking mist, but he made the assent fine. They looked out, wondering if they could see the approaching army that was coming to kill them all.

"Nothing yet," Eric said, straining his eyes.

Nathan raised a hand to shield the bright sun from his face.

"They will be here soon, don't you worry," Nathan muttered. He reached out for the brass gorget wrapped around Eric's neck, signifying his rank as a unit commander. He would be addressed as a captain from this time on. Nathan examined the plate gorget and the golden crown that was embedded upon it, front and back. "My son a captain." Pride exuded from his eyes and his voice.

Eric sneered at his father. "Me, a captain. I spent all morning trying to set up almost a thousand Elf and Dwarves who can barely understand me. Thank the gods Inda was there to translate."

"But you did it," Nathan smiled.

"Dad, they made me a captain. Captains lead one hundred men. I am doing the job of a knight with ten captains under him."

Nathan narrowed his eyes. "Eric, the King is busy. The ceremony for a knight is a tradition that takes time to perform," he said. "There is no doubt in my mind that you will be given a knighthood when this battle is over."

"Really? Do you really think that?"

"Yes, I truly do. King William is a good man. You will get a knighthood."

"After the battle. If I am still alive, you mean," Eric mumbled.

"Exactly." Nathan guffawed, slapping Eric on the shoulder. "Besides, we Bowman men serve our King for the honor and not reward."

Eric's face grew red as the heat filled his cheeks. "I haven't forgotten. I just want to raise my children differently than I was, is all."

"You grew up loved and well cared for." Nathan's tone grew defensive.

"I know, dad," Eric replied quickly, "I grew up good and safe, but I want my kid to be raised with a solid roof over his head, and maybe I could have enough money he could go to the capital, to the academy, if he or she so chooses to and get a proper education."

"The King's Educational Academy?" Nathan laughed, then stopped when he saw his son was serious and understood. "If that is what you wish for your children, then that will be fine, Eric." He paused for a moment, then added, "Is it Inda you wish to have children with?"

"Of course. She is the one I will be with forever." Eric sucked in a breath as he recalled the moon bowl and the vision of her lying covered in blood on the battlefield. He remembered not everything comes true that is shown. Glancing down, he realized the uniform he wore now differed from the one in the vision.

Nathan reached over and pulled Eric closer, hugging his son. Their moment ended when a Paladin rushed to the top of the hill. More Paladins came running up behind the first, and all looked outward. Warning horns sounded from around, and scouts came galloping out of the woods to the hill.

Duncan and Inda both came running. Inda found Eric and held his hand. He felt hers shaking. They watched for a moment when off in the clearing a line of black could be seen, then hundreds of Elf cavalry ran into the clearing from the woods.

"Well, Captain, there is no getting away from a battle now," Duncan said nervously to Eric.

Eric shook his head and swallowed the lump in his dry throat. "I did not come all this way to run away."

They stood on top of the hill for hours, watching the Elf army build their camp and place their pickets just out of range of the archers. They had built a palisade as if to surround the hills. King William and General Claiborne, who had arrived, watched closely.

"Surely, they do not mean to trap us up here and starve us out, do they?" Claiborne asked, shaking his head.

William smiled at his old friend. "I gave up trying to figure out what Elf commanders thought many years back." The King thought for a moment. "This is time they do not have. Winter will be here soon. They will have to capture Warriors Point before this area gets snowed in or return to Cyrworth."

Eric was standing nearby and took a few steps closer to the King, politely interrupting, "King William, sir."

The King looked at the Outrider, as though irritated at being interrupted. "Yes, Captain Bowman, what is it?"

Eric stepped closer. "I do not believe they want to spend months besieging us, sir."

"Well, what is it they are up to then?" General Claiborne asked.

Eric stood tall. "They want you to think they are going to starve us out, sir, but really, they merely want to stop you and Duncan from escaping."

William and Claiborne looked at each other, not following the Outrider. Eric continued, "Your highness, you have not seen the new magic used to the extent we have. The Druids want your and Duncan's blood. If Lirdjss gets either of your blood, she will become unstoppable."

"He is right," Inda said.

Duncan was listening as well. "Father, it is true. She spoke to me a few times when I was cursed. She told me she wanted my blood."

King William was silent for a moment while he let all the information sink in, then he let out a small laugh and said to Claiborne, "This magic stuff is over my head."

"That it is," Claiborne replied to his oldest friend.

King William turned and began leading his horse down the backside of the hill and shouted back, "Captain Bowman, come with me! We need to discuss a job for you and your unit of outsiders."

"Yes, my King," Eric shouted and ran after him.

16

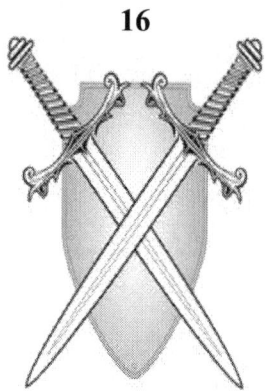

Darkness had come on. The Elf army was still busy building their siege works, with thousands of fires blazing. Eric was in an unfamiliar set of armor as he walked his horse to the gate on the west side of the hill. He was very uncomfortable in the armor, as it was not his.

He was wearing a set of the Elf dragon scale armor, and to make it worse, it was the armor of the Elf bodyguard he killed in the mountains; it stunk with the former owner's blood, and Eric cursed silently every time he took a deep breath in.

Most of the defenses around William's Hill were completed hours before the Elf army arrived and had given the men some time to rest and regain their strength after the forced march. As Eric walked closer to the palisade, he looked at Inda, who was apprehensive beside him.

"It will be okay." Eric said to her, trying to reassure her. "I am an Outrider. This is what we do." He then looked to his left and right at the thousands of human outriders and cavalry preparing themselves for the charge.

Inda shook her head at him.

"You are about to ride into battle, inside that encampment, where my sister could be sleeping."

"Yes." Eric smiled. "This is not the first Elf encampment I've ridden into in the dead of night. It's not even my second."

"Stop it, Eric!" Inda said, as she held his hand. "I should come with you!"

"You can't, and you know it, the Druid will feel you." He bent down and gently kissed her lips.

"That armor stinks." She pulled away.

He cringed again and cursed under his breath at the former owner, and wished he had killed him that night when they tried to take Duncan.

Eric climbed aboard his horse; the humans looked on with great hatred at the almost eight hundred Elf riders who mounted in front of them and all wearing their dragon scale.

Eric stared back at them in annoyance. "They are fighting for you as much as you are fighting for your homes. Remember that and don't forget to come when you see the signal."

Someone in the back called out, "Just make sure the pointed ears know whose side they are on this night, Captain!"

Eric did not answer the man. He simply ignored him and called for the gate to be opened, then slowly moved out with his Elf horseman behind him. He started at a walk, but then moved to a gentle gallop as he led them away from the hill and into the forest.

He moved deeper into the bush. More than once, he stopped, checking to see if he had been spotted and listened for enemy horns. They slowed their movement to be quiet as they moved. One enemy scout was picked off by the archers as they moved through the woods, then another. Apparently, Eric realized that the enemy Elf warriors were very apprehensive about shooting at other Elves wearing the same uniform as them and silently laughed as he thought this raid might work.

He kept his unit moving. It took them a long time to circle back around to the Elf encampment without setting off any alarms. Once they got close enough to hear them working on the fortifications, Eric let Gelvyr and most of the Elf warriors ride ahead of him in case a sentry wanted to speak to them, as they would surely come in contact with some.

They got closer, and as expected, they were challenged by some of the Elf sentries and a few human ones as well but, Gelvyr would speak to them, and they would quickly be let through. Once the unit would be almost by the sentry, he would be rapidly taken out, either with bow or sword.

Eric was shocked at how simple this was, and before he knew it, he was riding into the middle of thousands of dark Elf and human troops. Eric could hardly breathe. He kept his hood up over his head. He almost wished he would have stayed back and let Gelvyr lead this mission. But while Eric may trust Gelvyr and the light Elves, King William still had trust issues with them, and in his mind, they needed to prove themselves. So here Eric was, leading this suicide mission.

Thousands of enemy troops still steadily arrived into the camp—the confusion allowing Eric's unit to move around without suspicion. Eric had seen this confusion many times with large numbers of human troops in his time in the army. Organized chaos, he would call it.

When they were challenged to move, Gelvyr would simply speak to them and they moved on. Their targets were the finely made tents they had seen being erected from the hilltop when the camp first started being erected.

"No matter what army or kingdom or race they were facing, the elite never sleep in small tents like peasants." King William said when he briefed Eric on the mission, "Get inside with your Elves and kill all those in tents and do as much damage as you can, then retreat to the hill. We will cover you with a large cavalry charge during your escape."

As they approached the tents, which were easy to see with all the fires the Elf army had burned, Eric looked back at how far it would be for them to escape back to the hill. He quietly and nervously laughed at the impossible enemy-covered distance. His hands began shaking as he resigned himself to the fact he most likely would not make it back alive.

There were at least thirty large tents in the immediate area. Gelvyr looked back at Eric for confirmation it was time. Half of the Elves dismounted, as did Eric. He pulled out the Elf bow he had brought. He reached into the quiver of arrows that was strapped to the horse and pulled one out. This arrow was not regular. It had a small oil-soaked cloth on one end. He walked over to a torch burning nearby.

Eric knocked the arrow on the string, then touched the cloth to the flame and waited for it to ignite. Once it did, he drew the bow back and raised it to the air. His hands seemed to relax now. He pulled the string back to his cheek, then let the arrow fly. He watched as it travelled high in the air.

"I hope they see it," Eric whispered, knowing the signal arrow was small, and they were a long way away.

The dismounted Elves, casually trying not to raise any alarms, tiptoed into the tents. Eric instantly heard some commotion coming from inside the tents, but fortunately, the sounds of the Elves working on the siege works drowned most of it out. Eric took the torch burning in front of him and ran into the closest tent to him. He saw four bedrolls with four Elves sleeping in them. He looked at the armor that was hanging on racks beside each bed.

"Officers." He whispered as he pulled the Elf sword from his belt and stabbed the closet one in the throat as he slept. At that moment, the other three woke. Eric spun around and slashed the throats of two more before either could call out. The third one dove on Eric and wrapped his arms around him, taking him to the ground. Eric dropped the torch onto a bed. The two rolled around on the ground, fighting. Eric placed his hand over the Elf's mouth, preventing him from calling out. He looked over and saw the torch had ignited the blanket on the bed. Eric quickly reached over and grabbed the burning blanket and placed the flaming part over the Elf officer's face. He pressed it hard, letting the smoldering portion of the blanket burn and suffocate him as he held it. The flame went out during the thrashing of the officer. Eric held it in place until the Elf stopped moving. He kicked the body off to his side, and he quickly stood up with his sword in hand and left the tent.

Once outside, he found Gelvyr with a bow in hand, watching for anything. It did not take long before the ruckus in the tents began making others in the area take notice. Three human soldiers started walking over. Eric hated seeing humans in Elf armor, even more than he hated wearing it himself. Gelvyr waited for them to get closer and, with a very smooth movement, raised the bow and drew the string, the arrow that struck one of them dead in the heart, another Elf killed the other, and Gelvyr finished the third before he could do anything.

Suddenly there was a loud sound that sounded like thunder, and a tent was engulfed in flames. Eric spun around to see a Druid throwing fire bolts at his men. It was not Lirdjss or one of her four remaining Druids, but a regular one that had been signaled by a dying comrade.

The encampment was now being alerted. Gelvyr drew his bow and sent an arrow at the Druid, but it was easily deflected by an energy field. The Druid continued throwing fireballs until one of Gelvyr's mounted Elves got close enough to kill him with his sword. Eric laughed as the Druid thought the one that killed him was coming to his aid.

Eric ran for his horse and yelled for Gelvyr to call for his men to mount up. At that moment, an enormous explosion some miles away lit up the night sky. Eric looked to the east as a huge fireball seemed to climb into the sky as it made its way upward.

"Duncan!" He knew the King would now send the cavalry to his aid. Eric hoped and prayed they would put their hatred of his Elf warriors aside and charge.

"Move to the hill! Kill and burn everything on the way!" Eric screamed and pulled out a white scarf and wrapped it around his arm. His warriors all did the same, wrapping the bright white scarves or piece of white clothing around their arms, so they would be identified as friendly on their ride back to the hill. They all quickly formed a double line and moved forward until they were in a gallop.

Many Elves continued firing their bows from horseback as they rode forward, killing as they moved. Eric screamed a war cry as he drove his sword into the chest of a human soldier.

The confusion in the encampment only made things better for Eric and his unit. Bewitched men ran around confused, filling the night air with their demonic screams as they looked for something to attack. Some of the bewitched became so confused and desperate to attack something they even began recklessly charging at the hill alone.

Eric brought his unit to a full charge; they ran down hundreds on the way to the hill but were taking some casualties as well-aimed arrows began finding targets in his men. Druids set whole horses aflame along with their riders. Eric worries, as he knew they still had a long charge ahead of them to break out of the enemy encampment.

Eric had just sliced an arm off a human who tried to hit him with a spear when he heard a sound coming from the darkness, a low rolling sound. It was a moment before he realized what it was, a large unit of Elf cavalry coming at them from the west that, if not challenged, would slam into his flank and block half of his unit's escape.

Eric never gave it a thought and refused to leave half his unit to die and called for his men to turn and meet this threat. His men did just that and met the enemy's charge with great discipline, and a very bloody fight started.

They were now hung up in a tight battle. Horses screamed in pain and horror, Elf, and men cried out as they died. Eric slashed and hacked with his sword, killed as fast as he could, finding new targets until there were none in front of him. He turned to his right and was about to advance on some more enemy when he realized the rumbling sound had not stopped.

He knew it was more of his enemy coming to attack until he looked towards the hill and saw thousands of human cavalry charging in hard, with hundreds of Dwarves set on their rams, screaming insults and waving large axes in the air.

Eric cried out in joy and fury as the human charge mowed the enemy down as they met them. The confused humans and dark Elves now began running away in every direction. The smarter ones ran to the woods, but most just ran deeper into the encampment and were cut down as they moved. Those that remained did no better as they had not the numbers or any order on the field to stand properly, and thousands of the dark army died.

Eric looked to the west, where he had seen Duncan's fireball noticing more flames, but these were not red. They were green, large green flames that looked as though they were drowning out some red flames. Eric guessed some Druids tried taking on the Prince and failed.

The fighting went on for some time. Many Elf units tried counter-attacked but failed as the King's plan had played out perfectly. They burned everything they could before galloping back to the hill behind the trenched palisades.

Eric grinned from ear to ear as he led his men back to their staging area. Inda was waiting and handed him a water skin as soon as his feet hit the ground. He took a long drink, then handed the skin to Gelvyr, who gulped it the same as he had just done.

Eric looked at Inda and smiled.

"It worked, Inda." he said as he went to hug her, but she pushed him away. He looked at her, confused. He wondered if she was angry at him for killing so many of the dark ones.

"What?" He asked her softly, "What is wrong?" She said nothing, "Are you alright?" She pointed to his torso. Confused, Eric looked down and, seeing he was covered in blood, Eric laughed and began pulling off the armor at once. During this time, he did not notice, but he was being surrounded by his own Elf warriors.

Gelvyr walked up behind him as he peeled off the blood-soaked armor and tapped him on the shoulder. Eric turned to see him standing, and only then did he notice the several dozen Elves who gathered around him, a dozen or so carried torches. Eric looked to Gelvyr, wondering what was happening.

"Yes, what is it, Gelvyr?" Then looked around him again as the crowd gathered thicker. Many of the Elves were smiling while others stood watching proudly. Eric continued pulling off his armor until his chest was bare when he asked again with some concern in his voice, "Gelvyr, what is happening?" He then looked at Inda, expecting her to give him an answer.

"This is an honored Elf tradition." She smiled and walked away.

Eric then looked to Gelvyr confused, shrugged his shoulders, and asked, "So, what now?"

"Lay on your back. And leave your shirt off." Gelvyr said.

"What is going on?" Eric pressed, but Gelvyr said nothing as he pointed to the grass beneath Eric's feet. He reluctantly complied and laid down on his back, looking up at the stars.

Gelvyr smiled as he knelt over him, then looked to several of his warriors who were standing in the circle and said something in their Elvish tongue, and four of them quickly came forward and took hold of Eric's limbs and held them tightly. Eric gently pulled on their grip, but they were gripping him. He felt some fear run over his body as the unknown Elf tradition left him confused.

"Let me go!" Eric growled, but they held him firm.

Gelvyr was handed a knife with a wooden handle and a tiny blade by one of his warriors. After he examined the small blade that was no larger than his finger, he brought it to Eric's chest.

Eric's breath caught in his throat as the razor-sharp blade sunk into the skin on the left side of his chest. The second he felt it cut, he struggled to free himself and cursed at Gelvyr.

"Be still, Captain! This is a great honor," Gelvyr said.

"You best let me go, or I swear to the gods I will..."

Eric was suddenly prevented from speaking as another Elf knelt over his head and shoved a glove in his mouth. He struggled for another moment until he accepted the futility of it. Inda told him this was an honor, and he trusted her, so he stopped fighting and endured the pain until Gelvyr was done carving whatever was on his chest.

Eric watched helplessly as Gelvyr handed the knife off, then received a small bottle of what looked like ink, then poured the dark liquid over his wounded chest. Gelvyr then took the palm of his hand and ground the dark liquid into the wound repeatedly. Eric winced in pain as it stung, then winced again as Gelvyr took a hot, wet rag and cleaned off the access liquid from his chest.

During the entire event, Eric could hear the warriors about him praying to the moon and stars until Gelvyr's work was done and he was let go. He rolled to his feet only to fall down again as he was quite exhausted from the battle and this strange tradition. He struggled on the ground for a moment until he found his legs and stood looking at the proud warriors around him, who all seemed to look on to him fondly.

Eric was still confused and looked at his chest, hoping to see what had been done to him, but he could not make it out in the darkness. One Elf brought him a mirror, while the ones with torches came closer. Eric held the mirror in front of his chest and gazed at a very red and agitated patch of skin the size of his hand, where he made out the outline of an oak tree. The ink that Gelvyr had rubbed on made it easy to see. He looked to Gelvyr for an explanation.

"Eric, what you just received is an old ritual, an honor most Elf commanders would love to have, but few ever do, and many have died trying to earn."

"Why did you not just say that?" Eric looked at his stinging chest.

Gelvyr smiled. "It is an honor not to be asked for, Eric. It is to be thrust upon one. That is why there is the pain." Eric reached up and touched the tattoo on his chest as he understood. "Eric, these warriors have pledged their sword hand to you forever. They now trust you as their Captain."

Eric then turned to the surrounding group, looking at their faces. He was unsure what came next, but he knew he had to say something.

"It is I who am the honored one," Eric shouted, and Gelvyr translated.

Many of the Elf warriors came up and greeted him affectionally. After that was completed, Inda took him inside his tent and washed the blood off his body. She was even kind enough to use her healing powers to heal his chest, which left the tattoo looking perfect on him. He stood looking into the mirror at the tattoo, and the proudest feeling took over his body.

Eric quickly dressed in his own armor and walked back out of his tent to find Brandon waiting for him.

"Brandon." Eric greeted him.

"Captain Bowman, sir." Brandon laughed. "The King wants to see you immediately. I was sent to retrieve you, sir. He also wishes to see Inda and Gelvyr as well."

"Well," Eric grumbled, "We do not wish to disappoint his highness, do we, and it's me you're talking to, so cut out the sir stuff, will you?"

Brandon grinned and shook his head. "Duncan said I have to get used to using people's titles now that we're home. He said important people are easily offended."

"That they are." Eric nodded. "That is some sound advice that I must remember as well."

17

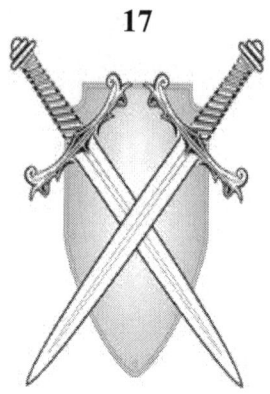

Eric, Inda, and Gelvyr were escorted by Brandon to the King's personal tent. It was a massive green and blue structure held high, with three poles in the middle. Two hundred people could easily be seated in it with tables and chairs, and a quarter of it was set aside for his living quarters.

A ten-foot-tall wooden palisade had been constructed around it with a step on the inside that currently had a dozen archers, guards, and paladins posted, keeping a close watch on the monarch.

Eric looked at the well-armed men who stood their watch, and every one of them nodded respectfully to Eric as he passed through the palisade gate and into the King's tent.

Once inside, he noticed it was filled with ranking knights, lords, and paladins. He saw his father and uncle were there and Grilrig, who had a plate of food in his hand. He smiled at Eric and took a large bite of a chicken leg he was greedily devouring. Corporal Talltree was standing back against the outer tent wall behind Prince Duncan, watching over him closely as he always did. As he stepped deeper into the tent, he noticed it had a wooden plank floor and was well lit with candles.

Everyone noticed their arrival. The crowd parted for them, making a path to the King who was standing at the front speaking to General Claiborne and looking at a series of maps on a large round table. Eric slowly made his way closer and waited for someone to tell him why he had been called upon.

"Well done, Eric. The plan you and my father came up with worked out well, and you came away with few casualties, I'm told." Prince Duncan joined him with a firm clap on the back.

"Yes, my Prince." Eric dropped his head to the Prince respectfully. They were not on the road anymore, and he knew royal protocols would have to be followed. "We got lucky. Unfortunately, the high number of officers and Druids we were expecting were not in our targeted area, but the damage we inflicted still made it a successful mission."

King William listened to Eric's brief, then stalked over. Eric knelt as the King approached.

"Thank you, Captain Bowman, stand, please." The King turned to Inda and smiled. He placed a hand on the shoulder of Gelvyr and nodded. "The plan worked better than I had hoped. Their encampment was left burning and covered with their dead."

"I had wished to find Lirdjss, my Lord, but she was not there."

"Not to worry, Captain Bowman. This battle is far from over," the King said. "I am thrilled with how your Elves worked out. Truly thrilled."

"I had no doubts they would prove good in combat, sir."

William looked at Inda and Gelvyr. "I am told it is because of you two the Elf cavalry defected to you in the mountains."

"Because of her, your highness," Gelvyr quickly replied.

King William nodded. "We will come back to that in a moment." He took his sword, which was sitting on the large map-covered table. "But first, we have something that needs to be done. Captain Bowman?"

Eric stared at the King, confused. A quick glance around. He caught his father and uncle off to the side, smiling proudly. Turning his attention back to the King, who walked over and stopped in front of him.

"Take a knee." The King commanded.

Eric fell ungracefully to the floor. He could hardly contain his excitement.

King William took his sword and held it with one hand over Eric's head, saying the words that had been passed down for over a thousand years all across Wreten whenever a man was given a knighthood.

"By the powers granted me by my father and my ancestors before him. I, King William Goodwin, in the presence of the brothers, do hereby grant this man, Eric Bowman, son of Nathan Bowman, the right of knighthood by the strength and honor of his deeds and by his bravery in battle." The King gently brought the sword down on Eric's shoulder. "On your honor, you will use this new right of power to keep the peace, protect the weak and vanquish the wicked wherever you find it." Eric's chest filled with pride. He felt his face fill with emotion, and he held back tears. He slowly looked up at the King and watched as the monarch finished the last of the ritual. "If you by chance turn to the darkness, may the brothers burn your soul." The King paused for a moment then finished, "Now rise Sir, Eric Bowman."

Eric stood up slowly. His hands shook as he held back tears. Though he rarely spoke of this, it was something he had wanted his entire life. He looked at his father, who was grinning ear to ear with pride.

Eric smiled and ended their moment with a nod. King William returned his sword to his sheath before leaning it against his chair. Then walked over and took hold of Eric's wrist and shook it firmly as he pulled Eric closer to him to whisper into his ear, "A knighthood should be taken seriously lad, and my son says you come from a line of honorable men, I have great trust in you."

Eric looked the King in the eyes and was about to speak when Duncan pulled him away from his father, and the two embraced like brothers.

"There is more to come, Eric, I promise. As soon as we win this battle, you will be granted lands and a castle," Duncan said.

Eric's mouth opened in surprise. "Really!"

"Of course! We will have to find you a squire." Duncan laughed, then let his friend go and stepped away. For the next several minutes, Eric was congratulated by many powerful men in the tent. He had no idea who any of them were.

The King shouted, quieting the rowdy crowd, "We have more honors to hand out." One by one, men's names were called of the remaining men who had accompanied his son north and brought him back safely.

Samuel was given a knighthood along with Davy, but Nathan was not, as he did not travel north.

Instead, he was made aid to the King himself for as long as he be needed.

"Always good to have old soldiers nearby, I say." King William placed a golden chain around Nathan's neck. It held the King's crest, giving him access to anywhere in the kingdom and to the King himself.

The King turned to Brandon, standing in the back, watching happily as his friends received their honors. Once the King found the orphan boy in the back, he waved for him to come closer. Nervously, Brandon walked forward and knelt in front of him. King William then called Grilrig and Gelvyr forward, who knelt beside Brandon.

"I am told the three of you have no home." He paused for a moment. "Brandon, I have been told you saved my son's life. In repayment for your loyalty, I grant you a special duty." Brandon's face lit up as he waited for the King to finish. "You will take a position as Sergeant of the Guard with one duty, that will be to protect my son."

Brandon smiled and looked around him as the crowd cheered.

The King then quieted the crowd again and turned to Grilrig, who was looking up at him calmly. "You, former Clan Lord, I heard you gave up your title for the good of your people." William stared into the eyes of the Dwarf. "A title you may not have been fully deserving of. Is this true?" William asked.

"I dishonored myself and my clan. I need to right that dishonor."

"Everyone makes mistakes, and some roads to redemption may take years. So, I will ask that you start here and stay on with my army and help Gelvyr with the Elf unit he and Eric are leading at the rank of lieutenant if you would accept."

"I would be honored, great King!" Then leaped to his feet held his ax high in the air, causing the crowd to laugh at the short warrior.

William then turned to Gelvyr and looked down at him. "And you, Gelvyr, I am told that you are a great warrior and leader. I ask that you become captain in my army and lead your Elf contingent in the battles to come. I give you my word you will be treated the same as any other unit I have in my army, and from this moment, your warriors will draw a wage the same as mine." Gelvyr said nothing, answering with a gentle smile and a polite bow of his head.

"Well, that is settled, then. Oh, one more thing. Inda!" King William said.

Inda left Eric's side, walking forward as everyone watched elegantly bow before the monarch took her hand.

"As of this moment, Lady Inda will be treated as a guest of mine. She will be given the honors of a visiting royal. After all, she is the King of Aethel's daughter."

A murmur rippled through the crowd.

Eric dropped his head as he wondered why the King would make that statement even though it was true and instantly worried for her safety.

"My father has a plan for everything he says and does, Eric. He will make sure she is safe." Duncan said reassuringly.

"I will keep her safe." Eric quietly replied as he remembered the vision in the moon bowl where he found her dead on the battlefield in the fighting that could happen any time now.

18

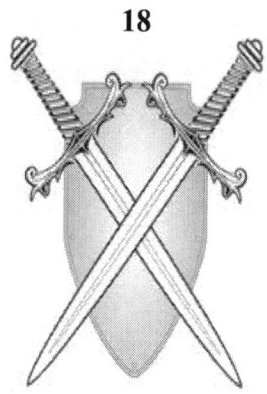

Four days had passed since Eric had been given his knighthood. He had expected that he would have felt dramatically different now that he was a knight, but in fact, he felt the same. He thought about it and wondered if it was because he did not dress like a knight and was not born rich like so many others. His uncle Samuel laughed at him when he had mentioned it earlier.

"Boy, what did you expect? A rich noble's blood is as red as ours, but we will never be accepted as one of them, even if we do become as filthy rich as they do. The only way we would be accepted as a noble is if we had been granted a lordly title."

"I guess," Eric replied disappointedly to his uncle and walked away, kicking at a stone that was near his foot. He made his way over to his horse, mounted the mare, and headed to the palisade that surrounded William's Hill that kept the massive enemy army out.

The bulk of the enemy's forces had finished arriving three days ago and had the hills surrounded. There had been daily skirmishes as the Elves probed at the palisade, looking for a weakness.

Eric reached the palisade wall that was closest to where they suspected the enemy leadership was camped. He dismounted his horse and climbed the tower that had been erected. Once atop, he greeted the two men at arms who were posted there, then looked out at the enemy encampment.

"By the brothers, they brought the entire Aethel army, didn't they?"

An older veteran with two crowns under his eye, a thick grey beard, and missing half his teeth that was wearing heavily plated armor, laughed. "Yes, one might think they have come intending to kill us all."

Eric matched his laugh. "Yes, one might think that."

"I heard the King gave you a knighthood." The old soldier enquired.

"He did." Eric replied proudly, "Some four days back."

"Well, that is good." The veteran slapped Eric on the shoulder before adding with the tone of pride in his voice, "They need more common-born stock to mix in with that uppity bunch and all their fancy clothes."

Eric laughed. "I won't disagree with you on that old-timer, but I am not sure about some of their fancy outfits." Eric turned and climbed down the ladder.

"Movement to the front!" someone yelled, followed by one of the army's Captains crying, "Stand to!"

The horns began sounding across the hills, bring the army to attention.

Eric looked out, and far off, he made out a group of ten riders coming directly for the palisade near the gates. Men came running to their assigned positions on the wall until they were filled with archers and soldiers.

The old veteran standing beside Eric laughed when the riders got closer and shouted, "They are holding a horse's tail! Looks like they wish to parlay."

"It looks like that, doesn't it?" Eric replied to him and watched closely as the Elf delegation stopped just outside the range of the archers. He looked at their fine armor, and he could see the sunlight glinting off the golden thorns that wrapped around their upper arms and shoulders.

Silence gripped the wall as everyone watched the ten riders on their mounts holding their position until the King and Prince Duncan arrived, followed by many knights and guards. King William climbed off his armored horse and rushed to the tower Eric was on, and climbed up the ladder. Once he arrived, the two veterans posted there bowed their heads, as did Eric, regarding the King.

"Thank you, lads, enough of that now." King William said to the men and looked out at the ten mounted Elves waiting for a human delegation and snarled. "It is the Elf elite, alright." He then looked at Eric. "Look at that fancy armor with the golden thorns they love to wear."

"Yes, my King, I noticed."

The King snarled again. "I guess we had better go see what they want to gloat about."

Several men standing close by laughed when they heard, and a young soldier only nineteen called to the King. "My King. Tell them we will not accept their surrender!"

More laughter was heard, and the King himself laughed out loud.

"Only if they agree to dig us some fresh latrines first." Men burst into laughter and cheered for their beloved King, who smiled with pride at their good morale as he made his way down the ladder and back to his warhorse. Climbed aboard, He looked back up the tower to Eric, who was looking down at him.

"Sir Bowman, are you up for a brief ride?"

"I most certainly am my Lord." He quickly climbed down the ladder, ran to his horse, and mounted the mare. The King watched Eric closely.

"Should we bring Lady Inda with us on this parley?"

Eric thought for a moment. "It would not hurt. After all, it was her presence on the mountain that brought the Elf cavalry to defect to us."

King William nodded, then looked at General Claiborne, who was on his horse, and simply raised an eyebrow at his old friend.

"If Lirdjss is with that group, Inda may be able to give us a different angle during the discussion. After all, they are sisters."

The King then turned his head back. "Brandon! Fetch Lady Inda. We need her for the parley."

"Yes, my Lord!" Brandon turned his horse, frantically galloping away.

Duncan then rode up closer to his father. He was holding a horse's tail on a spear.

"Lirdjss is with them, father." Duncan said with a shaking voice, and his father noticed how nervous the young prince was. "I can feel her power. She is powerful."

Eric reached over and placed a hand on the Prince's shoulder. "So are you, Duncan. I've seen you do things I never thought possible. Look how easily you killed that Druid on the mountainside."

"That was easy." Duncan said. "But that guy was nowhere near as strong at Lirdjss."

"Do that magic acorn thing again and make that whip." Eric shrugged his shoulders as though it was no big deal.

"I have some different tricks for this Druid, Eric." And both laughed until they heard Brandon's voice shouting behind them as he galloped closer, spurring his horse along.

"Make way! Make way for Lady Inda!" The crowd parted, allowing the boy to pass by with Inda riding her own horse close behind him. She was dressed in a set of light leather armor that looked a lot like the Outrider armor Eric was wearing, but would give her little protection. She had a small dagger on her left hip, and a leather satchel was strapped to her right hip. Her hair was tied up in the back, giving her a perfect ponytail that bounced as she rode. The outfit was topped off with her wearing a thin, light blue cloak attached to her armor with two golden broaches of an oak tree that matched the tattoo Eric had received some days before. The entire outfit made her look even more beautiful than usual, which caused many of the men around to stare at her in awe and lust.

King William called her over. "There is a parley party of ten waiting for us out there. I was wondering if you would accompany us to this meeting?"

"Are you sure, your highness?" Inda asked. "My presence may provoke my sister."

"I have never known an Elf to break a parley truce," King William replied. "But if you think it may, you can choose to stay behind." He added kindly.

Inda did not hesitate. "No, I will go."

"If anything happens, I will put up a protection field," Duncan said.

"You will not be coming, Duncan!" The King narrowed his eyes. "Nor will you, General Claiborne."

Duncan became furious. "What! I am going!" He took a deep breath in and calmed himself. "Lirdjss tormented me in my dreams and in my body with the curse. She could speak to me in my mind through the curse, father. I need to face her!"

"Both of us should not go out there, Duncan." King William looked at his son calmly.

"Then let me go." Duncan replied to his father, "You know, as well as I do, there will be very little in negotiations. This parley is simply Druid arrogance."

The King thought for a moment. "We will both go. I to wish to see this Druid who killed my son."

The King then chose the eight that would accompany them outside the palisade. Davy was the first to be picked with Eric and Inda, then he decided on two Paladins and three well-armed knights.

The gates were opened, and the party slowly rode out in single file but quickly made a long line to match the line the Elves were in as they waited.

Duncan held the horse's tail high in the air as they approached the position of the enemy. Eric reached over to his hip, pulled his sword out a few inches, and then set it back in the sheath. It always made him feel a little better, knowing the blade would come free easily if he needed it. He then looked to Davy, who was in his plate armor and always ready for a fight. Noticing he seemed much too calm as he rode. Inda was nervous, but Eric could tell she was trying to hide it. She looked back at him and smiled, to which he returned a wink.

As they got closer, Eric had no trouble finding Lirdjss. He looked at the center of the line and saw the female Elf with black hair and dark eyes, not unlike the eyes of the bewitched human that filled the Elf army. Her demonic eyes gave her a look of pure evil. Eric shivered. Her skin was pale white, her lips were blood red, her armor was much like the rest, but had more golden thorns. She also had a small golden crown of thorns that wrapped around her head, which held a glowing red crystal above her eyes.

King William stopped his horse three spear lengths from the Elves, and everyone else followed his lead. Duncan then stabbed the spear holding the horse's tail of truce into the ground beside his horse. This was then followed by the Elves, which caused a moment of silence.

Eric looked at Lirdjss closely and watched the rage build inside her as she glared at her sister among the humans. And it was the dark female Druid who broke the silence.

"Well, sister, shall we speak in the human tongue, so they can all understand?"

19

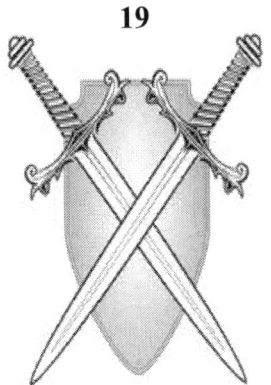

"I think that would be best, Lirdjss." Inda replied kindly to her sister, then added, "It does my heart good to see you." Eric watched and could tell that Inda truly meant it and still had a great love for her sister, but the kind comment was not reciprocated.

"Father will be very pleased when I bring you home to him in chains, sister." Lirdjss snapped. Eric shook his head at the Druid, which brought Lirdjss eyes to him and snapped with disgust, "Is there something you want to say, human?"

Eric politely looked to the King for permission to speak, which was granted with a nod. "You will not be taking Inda anywhere, that I will promise you."

Lirdjss laughed wildly, "Young warrior, I applaud your bravery even though it will get you killed."

Eric shifted in his saddle. He suddenly fought the urge to pull his sword and spur his horse forward to put an end to this Druid's arrogance, but self-control got the best of him just in time.

"Shall the parley begin?" King William asked.

Lirdjss laughed harder.

"Yes, oh great King, our terms are simple. We have you surrounded and hopelessly outnumbered. Surrender yourself and your son along with my sister, or you will all die." She leaned back in her saddle and gloated.

William said nothing and only looked at his son, who he knew was ready to speak.

"There will be no surrender, witch!" Duncan snapped. "We will fight you to the last. Your numbers do not scare us in the least!"

Lirdjss made arrogant threats while Duncan refused to let her speak over him and ranted about how she would lose the battle. Eric's eyes grew wide, impressed as Duncan purposely enraged the Druid. Eric noticed the nine Elves in her party watched at Inda with a fond curiosity. Inda studied each of them closely. He wondered if she communicated with them like she had done with others. He returned his attention to Lirdjss and Duncan, who thoroughly enjoyed making her angry.

"You are weak, Prince!" she screeched.

"No, I am not!" Duncan replied with a smile and reached inside his armor and pulled out his green crystal, letting the chain dangle it around his neck. He then made his eyes glow bright green. Lirdjss said nothing, though she tightened her grip on the reins of her horse as if she were about to run. But she stayed and stared at the green crystal as though her confidence had been taken from her.

Inda looked at her sister. "Yes, sister, I gave him the book. He is stronger than you will ever be."

Lirdjss turned to Inda and screamed, "Shut up! That is impossible!" Her eyes shifted from dark black to a bright glowing red, as though flames were going to shoot out of them. She then turned back to Duncan. "I will have your blood, Duncan! Like I told you before, I will drink your blood just like I did, your pathetic brother's!"

"I will have yours as well! Great King!" She shouted at William.

Eric could see King William struggle for a moment to contain himself when she had mentioned Simon, but kept himself from losing control. "My son was not pathetic, and it would be best you remember that dark Princess." He looked her in the eyes. "I've had enough. We will not surrender; therefore, we will end this on the battlefield!"

"Yes, we will!" She screamed as she turned her horse away and galloped to her encampment. She was followed by most of the Elves, except for two who stayed looking at Inda, who stared back at them. Then, after a moment, they too turned their horses and galloped away.

"Do you feel better?" King William turned to Duncan.

"No!" Duncan snapped, "But I want to kill her even more now than before."

"Are you strong enough to defeat her?" William asked Duncan, who looked at his father confidently.

"Yes, I believe I am."

King William then looked at Eric. "Is my son strong enough for this fight?"

"Yes, my Lord, he is."

Inda was listening and interrupted them, "My sister is not the real problem." Bringing everyone's attention to her, "The bigger problem is the army that surrounds us. Even if Prince Duncan can defeat my sister in the first moments of the battle, we will still need to defeat my father's army." She then gently spurred her horse and galloped forward and through the palisade gate.

They all watched her until she left their sight, and King William laughed. "Eric, you had better marry that girl. Even when she is frustrated, she is still beautiful."

Eric and Duncan both laughed out loud. "I was thinking the same thing, Sire."

"I have the perfect wedding gift for the two of you." Duncan said with a grin, "You will love it."

They all entered the gate, where King William rode directly to General Claiborne.

"We will not make another day without a major attack." William said calmly to his trusted General.

"The parley went that well then?" Claiborne asked sarcastically, bringing a smile to the King's face.

"I could see it in her eyes. It is blood she wants." William then looked around at the men who watched him closely, and then he gave a confident nod of his head, "We have good men here, but we cannot afford to be surprised. Make sure the boys are fed and ready." He gently spurred his stallion and rode away, followed by Duncan and his guardsmen.

"Do you think we have any hope, General?" Eric asked, remaining with the General.

The old soldier smiled at Eric and replied, "Come lad, you can help me see to the defenses."

20

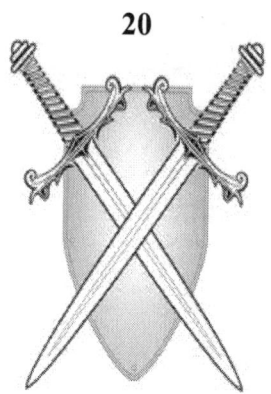

Eric had spent the day with General Claiborne, checking and amplifying the camp's defenses. It was well after dark before he had returned to his and Inda's tent. The night sky was clear this evening, and the moon gave a wonderful light, which made him feel a little better than it would help the sentries see anything in the darkness that would try to sneak up on the perimeter.

He had just handed his horse off to an Elf and was about to pull the tent flap open when he heard a faint sound on the other side of the canvas. Eric walked around to see Inda still in her armor, using the moon bowl. He stepped close to her, watching her, and smiled as the glow of the bowl gave the perfect shine on her face, bringing her beauty out. It took a second for him to realize she had tears running down her face. He remained silent until she pulled her hand from the bowl and dried it with a towel.

"What did you see?" Eric asked quietly. Inda did not answer him, as she used the towel to dry her face. He took her hands in his. "Inda, what did you see?"

"Our doom." She pulled her hands from his, taking the moon bowl back into the tent. He followed her inside and asked again, "What did you see?"

She turned to him. Tears filled her eyes again, and she wept. "We will lose the battle. It will happen tomorrow."

"You said yourself the moon bowl is rarely right when it predicts the future." Eric rolled his eyes. He stepped to her and tried to pull her into his body, but she pushed away and shouted.

"It showed me three outcomes of the battle, and all three are bad, Eric!"

"So, the bowl is wrong three times. We can still win Inda. Please do not lose faith. I have faced impossible odds in battles before and won. We can win."

She reached up and took the back of his head and kissed his lips. He pulled her into his body and wished his armor was off. She pushed away from him again.

"I need to do something, Eric," she whispered. "I will need you to let me."

Eric's face took a confused look for a moment, and he asked curiously, "Okay, what?"

Inda shook her head for a moment, not believing for a moment he would allow her to do what she was about to ask of him.

"The moon bowl showed me three outcomes of tomorrow's battle, and all three started the same way."

"Okay then," Eric said, waiting for her to tell him more.

"I intend on changing the entire course of the Elf battle plan, which will bring about a different battle entirely."

"If you are thinking of attacking pre-emptively." Eric explained, "The King has ruled that out. A defensive battle will be more beneficial for us as it will allow us to inflict more casualties than we will receive."

"That is not what I am thinking," Inda replied, and some tears ran down her face.

"Well, then. Out with it, what are you thinking?"

She lowered her eyes to the floor of the tent. "I am going to enter the Lirdjss' encampment and convince as many as I can to join us."

Eric said nothing. First, he just stood there staring at her like she had been touched by a case of the crazy before he snapped.

"Have you lost your bloody Elf mind?"

Inda rolled her eyes and turned away from him in frustration and embarrassment.

"You cannot go into their camp. The Druids will feel you, catch you and send you to your father in a box where I am sure he has a special punishment in mind for you!"

"It is the only way. I could tell at the parley many of the commanders, are conflicted. Now is the time!" Inda snapped back at him. Eric's face teared up quickly, and he walked to her and gently took her by the shoulders.

"I will not let you go. I love you more than anything, and I will not let you go, Inda. This is madness."

"I never thought you would, Eric." She then reached up, took him by the back of the neck, pulled him down, and kissed his lips. He returned the kiss and pulled her body closer to his. She began untying the straps to his armor, pulled on it, trying to get it off his body.

"This changes nothing Inda, you're still not going."

"Stop talking and take off your clothes."

Eric smiled at her as he bent over to pull off his boots. She reached for his head. He thought she would kiss him again, instead; she whispered a word in Elfish, and her eyes glowed blue for a second, as did her hands while she was holding his head, and Eric instantly fell asleep.

She gently set him down on the bedroll and positioned his body to be comfortable, gently kissed him on the lips, then whispered in his ear she loved him. Inda then stood and walked out of the tent, where Gelvyr was waiting for her.

"What did you do with the boy?" Gelvyr asked.

"He is sleeping. He will be up before dawn." She answered him sadly.

"He'll be angry in the morning. I bet he wasn't going to let you leave, was he?" Gelvyr said.

"No, he was not."

He handed her a horse and walked her to the closest gate, where several Dwarves were on guard with Grilrig.

"It is time, is it?" Grilrig said as he hoisted his large ax over his shoulder, walked to the gate, and ordered them to open it quietly. Nothing more was said; the gate was opened. She trudged out with her horse and did not look back. She mounted the horse and slowly trotted it away from the safety of the palisade and into the darkness.

She made her way slowly to the encampment. There were many more guards than she had expected, and it did not take long before she was seen. A voice called out from the dark, in the Elf tongue, for her to stop. She gently pulled back on the horse's reins, bringing it to a stop, and she replied to the Elf in the darkness.

"Do not alarm yourself, warrior, I am your prisoner now."

21

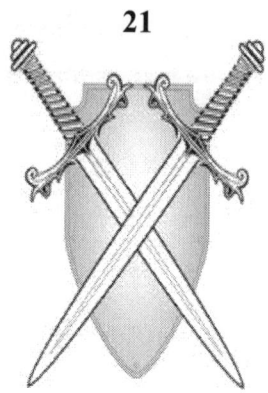

Eric awoke just as dawn was starting a new day in the world. The tent was black, as the small fire had burned out. He lay on the bedroll and thought of the night before. He did not remember going to bed. Eric reached over and noticed Inda was not with him. A strange feeling came over his body. A sense of dread, like a voice inside him, was telling him something was wrong. He then realized he was still dressed in his armor. Even in his boots, his sword was still on his waist.

He lay there in the dark and tried to remember until it all came back to him like a flash of light; he jumped from his bed and ran out of the tent looking for Inda and shouted her name, turning in circles, looking for her.

"She is gone, Eric." A voice came from behind him. He turned to see his father walk out from behind one of the three horses tied to a tree. "She left in the night. Gelvyr came to me and told me you may need me this morning." Eric stood frozen, looking at his father, unable to speak or show any form of expression. Nathan walked closer to his son. "You know she had to try."

"No! She didn't!" Eric bellowed.

Nathan took another step closer, to which Eric repelled with two steps back.

"She didn't need to try!" He pivoted and stalked to the horses and released the closest one, a light brown male with white socks. He untied the bridle and climbed aboard the unsaddled horse. "They should never have let her leave!"

He turned the horse around and galloped away, heading for the gate as hard as the horse could run. He was not sure what he was going to do, but Eric knew he was not about to sit around and do nothing.

It did not take him long to arrive at the gate. Grilrig and the Dwarves were still on the post, keeping a close eye out for any signs of Elf movement. Eric rode up to the gate and shouted for it to be opened. Grilrig stepped down from the palisade and walked over to Eric.

"You may be a knight lad, but King's orders say no one is to leave. We will fight a battle this day."

"Open the gate, Grilrig! Now!" Eric shouted at the Dwarf lieutenant, who showed him no mind.

"Sorry, my friend, King's orders."

Eric cursed Grilrig and knew there was no way he would get through the gate this morning, and felt helpless. He climbed off the horse, dropped the reins to the ground. Grilrig walked over and pointed to a small fire where two Dwarves were busy cooking on some large frying pans.

"Why don't you come and have some breakfast? We have a mountain of bacon, come Eric, eat with me and my men, maybe drink some of the hot beans this morning and take some of the morning chill off."

Eric knew it was hopeless and walked over to the fire and sat on a stump that had been placed there for that reason. A Dwarf placed a tin cup in his hand and filled it with the warm bean juice. Eric sat silent and stared at the steaming cup of black liquid for some time until he took a drink and felt the warm liquid slide down and hit his stomach to where it seemed to warm his soul.

Grilrig came over, sat beside him, and handed him a tin plate of bacon and warm bread with a thick layer of butter. "Eat it, lad. It will help." The Dwarf said almost like it was an order.

Two horses were heard galloping over, and it was Nathan and Samuel, both with worried looks on their faces, until they saw Eric sitting by the fire with a mouth full of bacon. They quickly walked over and were both handed cups of bean juice. They sat down and looked at Eric, who still said nothing.

"I was afraid you may have killed someone trying to get out." Samuel took a drink of the bean and winced at the bitter strength of it.

"I was expecting it with the look on his face when he arrived, but he calmed himself," Grilrig replied.

"Eric." His father nudged him to get him to look up from his plate. "Eric, look at me. I am sure she is alive. Prince Duncan told me her sister wants to bring her to her father."

Eric glared at his father.

"That does not help! How is that better?"

"It means after the battle today, maybe we can get her back," Nathan said.

Eric shrugged and shouted, "Look at the situation we're in. Do you really think we'll win this fight?" Eric stood and tossed his plate to the ground. "This grand idea of yours means we will have to win this battle against impossible odds!"

His uncle Samuel stood with him as though he was accepting a challenge and looked at his nephew.

"Well boy, if you want your girl back then I guess you'd better make sure we win this fight!"

"Oh, yeah Samuel, I will make sure we win this fight all by myself!" Eric snapped, then took a step closer, as though he would strike his uncle when a horn sounded off in the distance. It was heard again and again as it was relayed along the perimeter wall that circled the hills.

"Stand to!" Eric yelled as the soldier in him took over from the grief-stricken man, and he ran to his horse and mounted it. He said nothing else to his father or uncle and galloped away, back to his tent, where he had his own horse saddled and readied for him as he gathered his weapons and the rest of his armor.

Once he came back out of his tent with his helmet and grieves on his forearms and legs, he climbed aboard the loyal black mare that had served him so faithfully these past months. Gelvyr was standing next to his horse with his armor on and the reins of his horse in his hand.

"You know where our staging area is Captain, I will go for orders and meet you there." Gelvyr nodded to Eric as he spurred his mare and galloped away.

Eric rode hard to the King's headquarters. The entire time, he was trying to put Inda out of mind and focus on the upcoming battle that needed to be fought.

He arrived at the King's large tent and climbed off the horse. Men were standing outside, ready to hold horses, for important people in this battle would come and go. Eric had been made one of them by King William. The orderly took the reins of his mount without question, leading the mare off to the side with the rest of the horses.

Eric walked into the tent to find it jammed full of Lords, knights, and important older soldiers the King had trusted for many years. They were all standing in a large circle with King William, Prince Duncan, General Claiborne, and three other men moving small wooden figurines around a large map of the hills and the surrounding fields. He watched as a soldier placed some small figurines of what looked like catapults on the south side and dozens of wooden horses behind them, with an equal amount of small foot soldiers in front of them.

Eric stood silently back and watched as messengers hurried in with updates of enemy positions as they amassed their forces in certain positions outside the walls. Claiborne took a piece of paper from a messenger that had been hurried inside and quickly opened it, reading it before reporting to the King.

"It appears they will attack the east wall as well. They have amassed an extensive amount of heavy infantry there in the woods." Then took several wooden soldiers and placed them in their respective positions on the east side of the map.

"Well, we expected that. You placed Wilden's infantry on that wall, did you not?"

"I did," Claiborne agreed.

"Good, they will hold them. He has good men."

"Yes, he does." Claiborne agreed, then the two began discussing more plans and began issuing orders to the commanders in the tent, who left as soon as they received them hurrying to their positions and troops. Soon, the tent was emptying.

"Alright then." William shouted, "We cannot lead the battle from in here. We need to move to the high top where we can see the battlefield with our own eyes." The King shouted, then grabbed his sword and strapped it to his side. He gave orders for his aids to bring the maps and specific papers to the position he wished to view the battle from and stormed out.

The King had already mounted his horse before Eric had exited the tent and was galloping away. Eric grinned at the King's enthusiasm as he ran to his horse to catch up when he saw Duncan smiling at his father in the same manner.

"Well, your highness, your father still has the spirit," Eric said as they both climbed on their horses and tried catching the King.

"He is ready for this battle, that is for sure." Duncan replied to his friend, "I hope I am."

"It will all be okay, my friend," Eric said.

Duncan said nothing else as worry covered his face. Eric said nothing, for he knew what was bothering the Prince. He knew Duncan was scared he may not defeat Lirdjss sometime this day, or in the next few.

They galloped hard up the hill to the point where the King had viewed the battle from, and Eric was astonished at how good the view was from what King William had called the high top. He looked around from atop of his horse, where he could basically see the entire perimeter of their position. There were several points where one of the other hills came up and blocked the view of the palisade for certain parts, but it did not block the approaching grounds.

All the trees had been cut down for better visibility, and several towers had been built with the lumber and a small shelter where several tables had been placed, and the King's aids were placing the maps and papers, he had told them to bring.

Eric looked out again over the army's position and was impressed with the level-of-detail King

William and General Claiborne had prepared the military for this defense.

Eric then looked up at a perfectly blue morning sky and took a deep breath in, then told himself this was the last moment he would think of Inda until the battle was over. He then, for the first time, looked out beyond the wooden walls at the enemy army, and an icy shiver ran down his spine as he saw an unbelievably massive army taking positions to the south. Many tens of thousands of enemy troops in perfect square formation marching forward, then stopping just outside of their archer and catapult ranges. To the east, he looked where he could see thousands standing just outside of the tree line. Their black and red armor made them easy to see against the trees.

He let out a long, quiet whistle and tried to keep his nerve when he heard his father behind him. "Come on, boy, you have faced hard odds before, haven't you?" He turned to his father, wearing his new blue uniform with a grin on his face.

"They will sing songs of this day in the taverns."

"Win or lose," Eric replied with a grin. His father laughed, then trotted his horse over to the King, handed him a piece of paper, and then returned to his son.

"You must be waiting for orders?"

"Yes. I have the Elf contingent, the Dwarves, and three thousand light cavalry and Outriders waiting for a command to charge out and cause havoc," Eric said.

"Sounds like fun." His father gave him a fake smile, wishing he could hug his son, knowing the pain he was feeling for Inda.

"Fun. I want to fight!" Eric muttered.

The two looked out at the impressive yet terrifying horde preparing to take their lives.

22

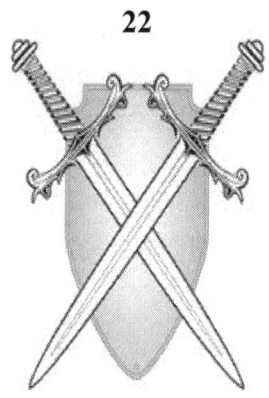

It did not take long for the Elves to begin their advance on the wall after they formed up. Eric looked down to the south and watched as the Elf army moved dozens of their catapults into range of the hill and began hurling large bucket-sized rocks and clay pots full of burning oil at the palisade, trying to clear the defenses and cause a breach. The King's army returned fire with their own missiles and stone-throwers, which were clearly crewed by men with better aim than their Elf counterparts. On their second launch, one human crew sent a pot of oil that landed directly on an enemy catapult and exploded into flames, igniting the Elf crew. The human defenders cheered from the palisade. While high upon the hill, Claiborne laughed.

"Good shots, those lads are."

William nodded in agreement with his friend, then looked at Duncan. The latter had moved away from the group and was sitting alone on the ground with his legs crossed and looked like he was meditating. His green crystal hung from his neck, glowing brighter than anyone had ever seen.

Eric was scanning the oncoming Elf ranks for any sign of Lirdjss or her Druids she had given the enhanced power to. He knew defeating them would be the key to winning this fight, but he saw nothing other than enemy troops. As he scanned the tens of thousands of enemy Elf and humans who had formed up around the hills, his mind continued to think of Inda. He tried focusing, but the emotional pain he felt was as intense as a sword sticking in his chest, so he sat on his horse and endured it, continuing to scan the battlefield. He reached down to his saddle and pulled up his waterskin and took a long drink.

"Sir Bowmen!" The King suddenly shouted, causing Eric to choke on his water. He took his water skin from his lips and coughed before responding.

"My King." Eric acknowledged, and as he spurred his horse, and moved up beside the General and the King.

"I want you to stay beside me. I want you to use your experience as an Outrider and inform me when you think the best time would be to charge your mixed unit out and get behind the Elf lines and cause mayhem." King William explained. Eric found this odd as he knew King William and General Claiborne had double the battle experience than he could ever have. Still, he did what he was told and began watching as the King explained more. "I want you to get through and disorientate their leadership, and hopefully, we will counter-attack in force with Duncan."

"Yes, my lord." Eric replied and began looking forward, then humbly asked, "I would like to send a rider to Captain Gelvyr and have him move my Outriders, Elves, and other forces closer to the west gate if that would be okay?"

King William thought for a moment. "That will be fine, send your father." Eric turned around and called for his father, who quickly came over. He gave his father orders, and Nathan was off at a gallop. Eric watched him ride away until his body had left the crest of the hill and out of his line of sight. He then shook his head, having realized the position he and his family were in. He was a young twenty-three-year-old common-born soldier sitting beside the most powerful man in the world and waiting to give advice to the King that could change the most critical battle in the history of Stalwart and all of Wreten.

"The gods' certainly work in mysterious ways," Eric said.

King William smiled, "Yes lad, they do."

"They most certainly do, Eric." Prince Duncan stood from the ground, his green crystal glowing brightly, as were his eyes. "You can set your mind at ease, Eric. Inda is alive."

Eric immediately felt a sense of panic and excitement balled into one emotion. His hands shook as he looked at the crown Prince. "How do you know!"

Duncan shrugged.

"Please Duncan, tell me!"

"I felt her presence when I was in the light. Unfortunately, that is all I felt and all I know, but she is not far away." Eric sat back in his saddle and let out a long breath and clenched his hands together. He felt the sweat on his palms, then wiped them on his thighs to dry them.

"That is good news, son." Said The king as he watched Eric.

"Thank you."

Everyone then turned their attention to the battle that was becoming more vicious just down the hill in front of them. Elf archers had moved closer and began firing volleys of arrows over the walls into the thousands of human soldiers who had been placed into position and covered themselves with their shields. The odd man cried out in pain as some arrows found a foot or an exposed limb. The human archers countered and fired their own volleys back. Catapults on both sides continued launching a combination of ordinances over the walls. The wooden palisades had given way in several spots as the large rocks smashed through the logs, creating the breaches the Elves were looking for and waiting to exploit.

The King, as well as everyone on the hill watching, knew it would be human troops the Elves would hurl in force at the breaches, a tactic they had used countless times in the past five hundred years. First, it would be the men they had bewitched with their dark magic. Then it would be the men they had conscripted. Only then would they send in their own kind, the elite Elf warriors who would fight with the discipline King William had said so many times he wished his men could conjure.

"There!" General Claiborne pointed forward to his left. "Human troops amassing there."

Eric then looked to the position where Claiborne was pointing. He could easily make out the poorly armored bewitched human troops who always found it hard to maintain any sense of a formation no matter how basic it was.

The King shook his head and said sadly, "It is always such a shame to kill so many humans who never had a choice on what side they were on."

"Father!" Duncan called out.

King William glanced over.

"Do you think this will work? If you are uncertain, maybe we should just let the archers kill the most of them."

"We won't know for sure unless I try," Duncan replied.

"I am not so comfortable letting them get in so close."

Eric listened, trying to make sense of what they were talking about, but not willing to interrupt the royals as they spoke.

"It will work, Father," Duncan replied, looking his father in the eyes, who then looked at Claiborne.

"What do you think, old friend?"

"Our heavy infantry can hold the breaches against the bewitched. I have no doubt of that." Claiborne then briefly looked at the battlefield. "I say let the boy try. Magic will be a major deciding factor in this battle, anyway. Best get on with it, I say."

William thought quietly for just a moment, then said to his son, "Go, earn your ink boy."

Duncan grinned and ran to his horse, and quickly climbed aboard. Davy and Brandon were behind him on their own mounts, as were a dozen more knights and Paladins, and all galloped down the hill, trying to keep up with the energetic young prince. King William smiled at his son as he hurried down the slope but, the smile soon left once the bewitched humans began advancing on the wall.

"The Elves are in a hurry today." Claiborne said when thousands of the possessed began their bone-chilling screeches and charged forward. "They only have a few holes to push through, but if they had waited a little longer, their catapults could have taken the half the wall down."

"Overconfidence," King William replied with a face of stone as he watched below. "They throw away humans like trash. Most of them won't even make it halfway to the wall."

"Hopefully, Prince Duncan's plan will work then," Claiborne replied, and Eric looked over at the King, wishing he knew what Duncan's plan was.

King William looked at Eric, noticed the curious look on the newly made knight's face, and smiled. "Duncan never told you his idea, did he?" Eric shook his head at the King, who then explained, "My son has it in his mind he can remove the possession spell the Elves placed on the bewitched humans. We know our Paladins have the power but, it is time consuming." King William stopped and looked at

Eric, who still had a confused look on his face. "Exactly!" The King couldn't hide the doubt in his voice. "Duncan says he can do it much faster and perform it on great numbers at the same time." He paused for a moment, looking at Eric, studying his reaction, then asked, "Do you think he can do it?"

Eric thought before he spoke, then remembered the battle outside of Dard when Duncan created a mist that brought on fear to whoever touched it, and he then replied to the King confidently, "I do, he has done similar acts, and he has only gotten stronger since then."

The King then turned his attention to the battle below and watched as the bewitched were now less than fifty yards from the wall. Archers had already begun cutting them down in great numbers. The enchanted continued charging with no fear whatsoever, and a second wave was sent through the wall.

The proud King readjusted himself nervously in his saddle. "I should have sent Duncan back to Cardin."

23

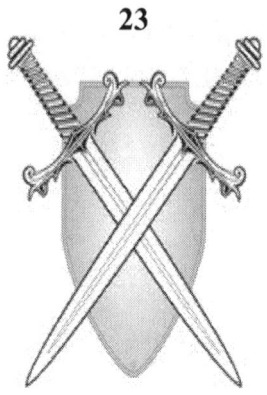

Duncan and his party reached the outer wall. He quickly dropped from his horse, ran to the closet tower, and climbed the ladder, followed closely by Brandon. The Prince had ridden to the area covered in flames from the Elves' incendiary ammunition they had been hurling in. The wooden palisade that protected their position had six gaping holes in it, from the incoming boulders that had sheered some of the six- and eight-inch logs off like a sharp sword to a candlestick. Men were piling logs and rocks in the holes, trying to fill them with anything before the bewitched pour through them.

Duncan had reached the top of the ladder where he stood alongside two armed men with spears waiting for the enemy to come into range and watched below as the Stalwartian archers along the wall fired into the advancing bewitched, killing them as they charged.

The terrifying screeches of the thousands of possessed were bellowing so loud Duncan had to fight the urge to cover his ears, but he simply closed his eyes and went inside himself, finding the warmth of the light.

Brandon stood bravely beside the Prince, holding his round shield across Duncan's torso, protecting him from anything that might be flung at them. Duncan focused carefully, then opened his eyes, which glowed green like an emerald in the sunlight. He reached forward and pushed Brandon's shield away, and then shouted to his archers to stop shooting. But the screams of the bewitched were much too loud, and the men continued with the killing.

Stalwartian heavy infantry ran to the gaps in the walls with their long rectangle shields and spears. They used their bodies to plug the holes in the walls as they placed their shields together and pointed their spears forward. Brandon watched Duncan as he brought his hands close to his chest and whispered some old words in a language he did not understand. The Prince's hands began glowing green just as his eyes were, then a green light began filling the space between his figures. The two men on the tower started throwing their spears down at the bewitched as they neared the wall. Soldiers braced themselves for the coming collision.

The bewitched screeched even louder. The Stalwartian heavy infantry bravely called out their war cries as the two armies made contact in the palisade gaps. The bewitched ran directly into the spears of the defenders, then fell to the ground. The brave soldiers stabbed and pushed on their shields. The men behind them stabbed with their own spears over and between their comrades.

Davy and the rest of the Prince's guard stood at the bottom of the tower in formation as if the shield wall broke. Davy shouted out encouragement for his brothers as they fought for their lives and wished he was with them.

The light in Duncan's hands was now so bright Brandon thought the Prince had conjured a piece of glowing green glass. Duncan then took one step forward and tossed the brilliant piece of green light as though he threw a ball forward. Everyone watched as it made its way through the air, then fell to the ground and exploded, causing a ripple of green light to move outward in all directions, like a wave after one had thrown a stone into a calm pond.

The wave moved outwards with astonishing speed through thousands upon thousands of bewitched, causing each it touched to fall to the ground, screeching their demon rage as though every one of them was in agony until it covered the entire horde of attacking bewitched men. Their eyes, which were always like black glass, began glowing green.

Brandon listened as their screeches began changing to the cries of a mortal man in pain. The Stalwartian defenders atop the walls stopped shooting them, the heavy infantry stopped killing them, and the battle on both sides just stopped.

Duncan quickly left the tower and made his way to the closest hole in the wall, pushing past the infantry, blocking the holes. Brandon and Davy followed him outside the wall amongst the men whose cries of pain were easing.

The Prince stepped over several men who appeared to be weeping, not from pain, but from the relief of the torment they had been under. Duncan reached down and helped a man dressed in nothing more than leather pants and a tunic. He looked into the man's eyes and saw no darkness, just the tear-filled blue eyes of a man from the far east and his long blonde hair.

Many more of the former bewitched men stood, most with weakened legs. None picked up their weapons. Most were still sobbing. It was then Duncan noticed the dead silence that descended over the battlefield.

Duncan stepped back against the wall and asked for a horse that was brought to him immediately and he climbed aboard so he could see the formerly bewitched men and wanted them to see him. Duncan looked at the men with pain and sorrow in their eyes. Some had great fear in them, like he had never known himself. The Prince then shouted to them.

"You have nothing to fear from the Elf Druids anymore! We can match them with magic. We can match them with the skill of arms." Duncan then took a deep breath in and continued, "We can save your people if you help us. The Druid can no longer possess you again. My spell is protecting you." Silence continued to fill the air.

A man who had been on the tower with him shouted, "Prince Duncan. Movement Sir! Movement on the Elf lines, Sir."

Duncan then looked back to the tower at the soldier who was pointing forward, but he was unable to see what the soldier was pointing at, so he shouted up, "What is it?"

"Looks like the Elves are sending in the human infantry, sir, not more of the bewitched, but the conscripts, sir."

"Very well!" Duncan shouted. He then turned his attention to the former bewitched and called, "Pick up your weapons and join us, or make a run for your homes. The choice is yours!"

The enemy catapults began firing again, pots of burning oil began landing in the crowd of the confused humans who seemed to take that as a sign of what was to come. Most immediately reached down and picked up their weapons and began cheering for the Prince. A few tried to run away but were cut down by the Elf arches as soon as they came into range.

"Form up!" Duncan screamed, and the newly freed men began forming up on the outside of the walls. Duncan dismounted his horse and ran to the front rank with his bodyguards, Davy and Brandon beside him and Davy protesting his choice of tactic and pleaded with him to get behind the wall. The Prince ignored him and made his way to the front of nearly eight thousand newfound allies.

A knight behind the walls led out his two thousand heavy infantry units and formed them up behind the poorly equipment freedmen.

A few dozen Paladins ran forward and used their protective fields to surround Duncan and his new army in light and waited for the next wave of attackers, whether human or Elf.

24

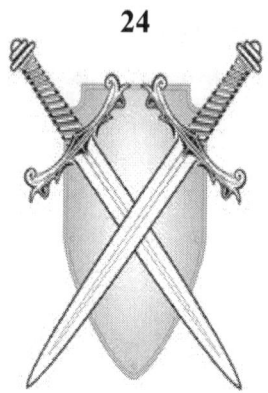

"What is that boy doing?" King William shouted, "Standing out front of thousands of men who he does not know if they will turn on him or not! A moment ago, they were all bewitched!" He squirmed in his saddle, looking down at the events below. "By the brothers Claiborne, please, tell me what he is doing!"

"I wish I knew, Sir." General Claiborne said with a smile, "But he seems to have inspired some of the heavy infantry. They are pouring out to fight with him and our new allies by the looks of things."

"They all need to get back behind the walls! He may be my son!" He raised his fist in frustration, "But this is still my army!" He looked at the enemy human infantry, who were in a less than perfect formation, slowly marching forward with rounded wooden shields in red leather armor and round helmets, then quietly cursed under his breath.

King William had faced these enslaved humans many times and had never lost to them. Often, they quickly broke ranks and ran. Many surrendered to be taken prisoner, but there were always some who would choose to fight, and this time, his son was standing in the middle of over five thousand men whose loyalty could not be guaranteed.

His royal highness cursed again, louder this time, as he looked around for a runner when he saw Eric beside him. "Eric!" He shouted, sounding desperate, "He might just listen to you, get down there and have Duncan move back inside the walls. We can't lose him and have Corporal Talltree, I mean Sir Talltree, take command of the bewitched unit. Do you understand?"

"Yes, my King." Eric quickly replied, then galloped down the hill as fast as the mare would take him. He pushed her hard down the hill and into the short distance to the wall. Eric passed several catapults and their crews as they let fly pots of oil and large rocks at the conscripted humans who were advancing. He saw the hundreds of archers on the walls preparing their bows. Younger, mostly boys, ran about with quivers full of arrows and spears, making sure no one would run out.

Eric rode his mare through the breaches in the wall and galloped her around the massed formerly possessed troops whose spirits seemed to grow. Some were still weeping, but many seemed happy. Eric could only think it was from the torment they had been through, with some form of a demon taking control of their body and being held captive inside their own mind.

"Maybe they will fight," Eric said, surprised. He followed the royal sigil flying on a banner to the middle of the formation where Duncan was drinking water with Davy beside him, shouting orders to the men about him and encouraging them that the Prince was going to fight with them and that they would be the first to bring down the Aethel empire.

A large rock came flying in and landed near the front of the line, and dug deep into the ground, causing a sizeable amount of dirt to be flung high in the air. Eric's mare reared in the moment, but quickly settled. "Duncan!"

"What is it, Eric?" Duncan answered.

The thousands of men around the prince were excited and very loud. Eric was forced to yell for Duncan to hear him. "Your father wants you to get behind the walls. He does not want to lose you."

"Please tell my father that I know what I am doing and that I must draw out Lirdjss quickly and defeat her to save our army. This is the only way."

"By getting yourself killed?" Eric shouted to him, "Your father has ordered it, Duncan. Davy is to take command!"

"You are my friend Eric, but I gave you an order to bring a message to my father! Now move!" Eric pulled back on the reigns and backed the horse away. He understood Duncan's tactic, but his father was the King, and Duncan was merely a Prince.

"I will do what I can for you," Eric said and turned his horse, following the same route back up the hill to the King and reported the Prince's plan, and waited for him to respond.

"He is trying to draw the Druid out?" Claiborne asked, wishing to clarify.

"Yes." Eric answered the general, "I believe his plan is to kill her here in the start and save the army."

"Well," Claiborne grumbled, "Why did he not tell us of these plans before the fighting started?"

"Because he knew I would have said no." William replied calmly. "The boy will not listen to me, will he, Eric?"

"No, my King, he is too much like you, Sir, strong-willed."

The King sighed. "Is sending Eric back down there with some of my best knights and forcibly carrying Duncan behind the wall an option?"

Eric laughed. "Sure, if you want Duncan to curse them all to lose control of their bowels right there on the battlefield, or maybe he can cause a vine to shoot out of the ground and tie up your knights." Eric grew serious. "I've seen him use his powers in battle. If he doesn't wish to come, he won't."

"I never should have let him come up here with us! It is much too dangerous for both of us to be here!" The King shouted in frustration, then calmed himself. "But since I did, I will trust the boy. I have no other choice for now."

They returned their attention to the battle and watched as the enslaved humans stalked towards the Prince's position into the range of their archers, who immediately opened fire on them, sending volley after volley raining down on the attackers.

Eric looked to Duncan's position and watched as a glowing ball of green flame left Duncan's hands and flew into the ranks of the attackers. This was followed by Paladins, who began using their smite spells that had served them so faithfully in the past, sending bolt after bolt into the enemy. Duncan sent several larger balls of green flame into the ranks of the enslaved, and, like expected, they broke and run even before they had gotten within forty yards of Duncan's position.

The formerly bewitched men cheered as the forces belonging to the Elf army broke and ran. Eric watched as they all retreated to what they wished was the safety of the Elf position out of range of the powerful Prince and his archers and Paladin. Their wishes were not granted as Elf archers and Druids began firing directly into them, killing without mercy for what Eric could only guess the Elves called cowardice. He watched, and for the first time in his military career, he felt sorry for his enemy, who had nowhere to go and formed up inside squares with their shields around them and walked to the middle in between the two armies.

When the enslaved men first advanced on the hill, they came with about eight thousand men. Now stuck in the middle, they had less than five huddled together, seven in large squares with shields on all four sides and over their heads.

"Smart. They formed the turtle," Claiborne said.

"They can't survive there for long with the Druid launching their spells at them." The King replied with some sympathy for them, "I am surprised Duncan has not tried to entice them to join him."

"It looks like you spoke too soon, sir." Eric pointed down at Duncan, who was surrounded by at least fifty Stalwartian men and at least a hundred of the freedmen. They were running forward until the humans were in their voice range.

Everyone on the hilltop watched as Duncan's forces called for the humans to join them. The thousands of freedmen in the back beckoned them and waved for them to run to them. At first, nothing happened, but then one man with short black hair broke free and ran north, then another, then ten, a hundred, and finally thousands fled to the prince leaving only a few hundred hanging back who all ran to each other and reformed into a single turtle.

Duncan brought them back and formed them up into his ranks in front of the first group of defectors, many smiling with joy. Others had a look of dread on their faces, but all looked to the Prince for leadership.

"I cannot believe that just happened," Eric muttered. Looking on, the King laughed as though he just got the punch line of a bad joke.

"He's giving them hope. Duncan is giving them hope that maybe the Elves can finally be defeated. That's why they are defecting."

"Glorious," Claiborne replied, then turned back to the battle.

Minor skirmishes had broken out along the wall on the other side of the hill, nothing more than probes, while the main body of the Elf army to the south had pulled themselves back out of range of the King's catapults. Soon smoke was seen deep in the enemy camp. Claiborne pointed out was coming from one of the many human encampments.

William then looked to Claiborne with interest and asked, "You don't suppose they are killing the rest of the human troops they brought, do you?"

"To an Elf, it would be the smart thing to do after what has taken place this morning," Claiborne replied to the King.

William then looked at Eric. "What do you think, Outrider?"

"If I were an evil Druid, I would attack and kill every human I had nearby." Eric faced forward and added, "I wish Inda was here with us. She would be an excellent source of info right about now."

"I agree." The King nodded.

25

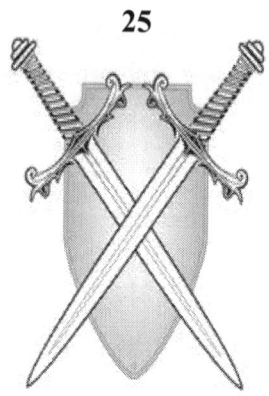

Inda was sitting cross-legged on a blanket inside a large tent, her hands were bound with chains behind her back, her clothing had been forcibly removed in the night, and she was given a thin white robe in its place, which did little against the cool fall air this morning. She had not been harmed yet and counted herself lucky for that, as her sister was very unhappy to see her arrive the night before. The sentry she had come upon was a loyal young Elf and brought her directly to his commander, who quickly reported it higher. She had been bound, gagged, and even hooded until she was placed out of sight in the tent where her sister had verbally tormented her half the night.

The large tent flap had been tied back, and four of Lirdjss' personal guards had watched her closely all night, making sure she did not speak to anyone. Normally, Lirdjss would have gloated and humiliated her younger sister in public and let everyone know how much power she had over her, but last night, her presence was clearly kept a secret.

After Lirdjss had finished her tirade and berating Inda, she left her alone with the guards, where she placed herself in a deep meditative state and brought forth the light and used its warmth on her exposed feet and lightly clothed body.

Hours ago, she had heard what sounded like thousands of troops moving past her tent. Now the fighting in the distance seemed to move closer. Perhaps King William had launched a pre-emptive strike, as they had done a few nights ago. The sounds of the fighting had died down considerably now, except for the odd moan of the wounded.

She wished she had her hands free so she could help the wounded. Inda had tried asking the guards if she could help, but none would acknowledge her. She sat on the blanket and went back inside herself to the warmth. Earlier she had felt the presence of Prince Duncan and tried to speak to him, but failed, as he was too far away.

She hadn't long to wait before her boredom was interrupted when Lirdjss stormed into the tent in a rage. She struck her across the face hard with the back of her gloved hand, sending Inda to the ground.

"You taught the Prince this magic!" Lirdjss screamed almost uncontrollably, "You fool! He caused many of our human troops to defect and removed the spirit curse from most of the possessed!" She then stepped to her sister once again, kicked her in the stomach with her thick soled black leather boot, and then kicked her again. Inda lay on the ground fighting for air, but inside she was proud of Duncan. She did not know he was planning a mass exorcism or even knew he could do it.

"You taught him that, didn't you?" Lirdjss asked, panting from her exertion, "To remove the curse."

"No." Inda replied as she finally regained some of her breath, "Only because I never thought of it." Then she could not help herself and smiled, but pushed her face down into the blanket, hiding her expression to avoid another boot to her torso.

"I hope you are happy. Your friend caused us to attack most of the human units we had with the army." Lirdjss paused for a moment as she enjoyed the shock on her sister's face. "Oh, not all of them, dear sister, just the ones we knew could not be trusted. Some we know are loyal to our father." Then with that, she kicked Inda in the stomach again, bent down, and picked her sister up into a sitting position, then sat beside her and whispered into her ear, "I've heard rumors, Inda."

Lirdjss calmed herself. "That you have fallen in love with a human." Inda said nothing. She just looked down, which brought out Lirdjss' arrogance again. "You always felt too much for the humans, my sweet Inda." Lirdjss reached over, and with one finger, she gently slid Inda's hair back behind her pointed ears. "I bet he is handsome. Is he handsome?" Inda still looked down, saying nothing as her sister continued, "I am told his name is Eric Bowman, an Outrider."

Inda then lifted her head, looking at her sister. "No!" she snapped. She knew the reason Lirdjss had gathered information about Eric.

"I am not surprised you picked an Outrider; they are the strongest. They are the best, I am told." She paused for a moment, then arrogantly added, "If he survives the rest of the battle, I will have him burned alive so you can watch."

Inda lowered her head and quietly asked, "Sister, why are you so in love with inflicting pain?"

"It gives me pleasure, dear sister. Inda, I have grand plans for you and your human friends, your traitor Elves, and your Dwarf dogs. Sister, news of

Prince Duncan's powers has spread to the humans across Wreten and brought hope to the human population." Her voice changed to anger again. "They are rising once again all over the empire." Lirdjss stood up and looked down at Inda, her rage returning. "but even more important, little sister; is news of your return has been spreading, and some Elf units have joined you. Now the peasant class of our people is becoming restless." She took a short step back, then shouted, "And it is your fault!"

She kicked Inda in the stomach, again and again, shouting the entire time. "I am going to brand your naked body in front of my army, sweet sister, and show the peasants there is no hope."

She stopped kicking and knelt again, then slowly lifted Inda back up, who was gasping for air like it would never come. Lirdjss reached down and placed her hand on her sister's stomach and used her power to bring her sister some relief before continuing calmly.

"And after I drink Prince Duncan's blood and bring his pathetic father home for our father to drink his blood, we will use that strength to destroy what is left of Stalwart, find Duncan's precious sister, and force her to have babies so their blood can fuel more Druids. Then we will have all the power in the world for the next thousand years."

Lirdjss dropped her hand, rose, and stalked out of the tent.

Inda watched her walk away. She stared at the guard, who stood by observing.

"Did you hear that, young warrior? The next thousand years."

The young guard dropped his gaze to the ground as the shame filled his face.

26

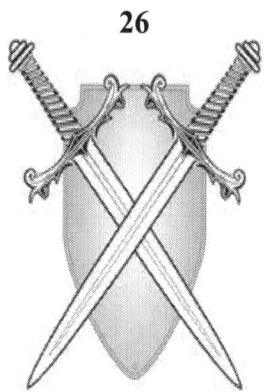

Eric was still up on the hill waiting for orders from the King while he watched the events below. The smoke in the Elf encampment had increased, and there were more signs of internal carnage increased by the moment. Eric wished he could see better, but that was impossible, as most of the Elf encampment was too far away and in the forest. More and more humans had left the Elf ranks and were pouring out of the woods, defecting to Duncan's position. It did not take long to realize Lirdjss had given orders to slaughter most of the humans they had conscripted into their army. Claiborne laughed when events at the enemy position had come clear.

"I must buy Lirdjss a bottle of the finest wine. She destroyed a third of her forces for us."

The King grunted, "She still has us almost two to one, but maybe I will send her a bottle from my private stock. Madness in an enemy commander can be a wonderful ally in a war." Then he returned his attention below and watched as hundreds more humans ran to his son's position outside the walls.

Soon, the Elf cavalry began attacking the humans as they fled for safety. King William watched closely as the defectors fought bravely for their lives, and just what the King feared, Duncan led men forward to cover them. "That boy!"

"He will be okay," Eric said, hoping he wasn't speaking out of turn. "But if I would, my King, you asked me to tell you when, in my experience, I would lead my Outriders out, sir. A charge below us on the right, sir."

The King looked below and studied the terrain and situation. "Yes, I think now would be good timing, lad."

"Yes, my King, the confusion directly forward of us is perfect, sir. Also, I would like to have my charge led by some heavy cavalry as well."

"I will have Sir Martin and his heavy cavalry meet you at the west gate. Once outside, quickly form up and charge south. Try to disregard any Elf units that may try to harass you on your charge south."

"Yes, my king." Eric snapped like a loyal soldier and began turning his horse away from the King.

"Expect an infantry charge to come in behind you if your attack is successful." Eric nodded to the King and galloped away.

Eric rode hard to his unit, and once there, he found out that Gelvyr had them ready to ride. The Elves were all lined up in a rank of three, standing beside their horses in their armor, with the Dwarf unit behind them. Two thousand Outriders were lined up in the same manner beside them, ready to ride at a moment's notice. Cheese and six more Outrider officers were standing with Gelvyr at the front, prepared to receive Eric's orders, as was Grilrig, holding his large ax, who smiled when Eric approached.

"Well, since you finally joined us, may I presume we will get off of our backsides and get into this fight?"

"You may." Eric climbed off his horse and gave them a quick briefing. "Sir Martin's heavy cavalry will lead the charge ahead of us and help us break through the Elf line." Eric turned to Cheese and the other Outrider officers and said, "Once through the Elf line, spread out and do what we Outriders do best, create chaos until the infantry arrives."

"Sounds simple enough." Cheese shrugged. Not a minute later, fifteen hundred heavy horses could be heard coming from deeper inside the hills to the western gate. They were led by an older, well-known Knight, who had three crowns under his eye and a deep scar under his other. He had a red horse painted on his shield.

The forty-eight-year-old climbed off his horse and grunted when his feet hit the ground. He pulled off his helmet, allowing his long black hair to fall down. It was full of knots, like it had not seen a bath in months. Sir Martin looked at Eric and wasted no time.

"Sir Eric, the King says I am to take the lead on a charge with your men behind us to allow you to break through the Elf lines."

"That would be correct, Sir."

Sir Martin was a man of little patients in war and looked at Eric's men. "Well, give me the details and let's get at it then, son, the war is awaiting."

Eric gave him a rundown of how the attack would proceed, and Sir. Martin agreed with the plan but then added,

"Make sure my right flank is protected during the charge. We do not know what might come out of the trees as we charge south along the wall. It will be you Outriders who have the speed to get into position, so it will be up to you to protect my right."

"Agreed." Eric replied, then added a line from an old prayer, "May the brothers protect us all and grant us a swift victory."

Sir Martin smiled and added, "May the brothers shroud us in their armor and make our flesh as of the metal of the gods."

Nothing else was said. Every man, Elf, human, and Dwarf mounted up, placed on helmets, and moved as close to the west gate as they could. Sir Martin looked back and lifted his lance high and shouted,

"Open the gate!" The guards quickly pushed the gates open, and the heavy cavalry, with their long shields, galloped out and turned south as soon as they cleared the earthworks and wall. Sir Martin kept them tight against the wall and held his column at an easy gallop, allowing his men to come up in a long line of twelve broads. Once they cleared the south wall, they would spread out wider. But for now, he wanted them against the wall to allow the archers to give them cover against anything that might come from the forest at them. He looked behind him and saw Eric leading several hundred Outriders to his right, placing them into position to ride forward and cut off any attack that he feared. "Damn good lad that Bowman."

Sir Martin picked up the pace of his men, doing it slowly so they could keep their formation. He looked to the west, and nothing was happening yet. He picked the pace up once again. Soon they passed the south wall and were in the open. Sir Martin raised his visor and looked to the man riding beside him, and nodded to him. A young, twenty-three-year-old raised a metal horn to his lips and sounded the attack formation signal. The musical note of three short toots and two long told the entire fifteen hundred riders what formation to proceed into. Like practiced dancers, they rode their horses into line one hundred long in fifteen separate lines and spread themselves out so they would not trample each other.

Martin looked at the man beside him and lifted his lance high, and nodded again. The rider raised the horn to his lips again and blew one long note with two quick ones at the end, and fifteen hundred men spurred their war horses onward and let out a battle cry loud enough to wake the brothers.

Martin directed his charge to the position on the Elf line just to the right of where the humans were still defecting from. To the left, the Prince and his men were pushing forward. To the right, and saw a contingent of Elf cavalry coming out of the forest to intercept and disrupt his charge. He then noticed Eric galloping forward with several hundred Outriders to prevent them from their mission.

Sir Martin grinned in his helmet as his confidence grew and shouted, "They can't stop our charge now! Nothing will stop us now!" Sir Martin laughed out loud. He lived for these moments like these gave him a reason to live, his body filled with excitement. As he galloped, he watched forward as the Elf line came closer and closer. He could see there was a sense of disarray amongst the Elf units. They were not in the perfect formation they usually were in. The sight of this gave him even more excitement.

"We will ride them down like flowers!" He shouted while his men continued their war cries.

They approached their target with their horses at full gallop now. Sir Martin had several paladins in his ranks who began sending in smites ahead of the charge, which created even more confusion for the Elves. Some even broke and ran. They were less than a stone's throw away now. Some Druids sent fire bolts into the charge. His men screamed in rage and fury again.

Sir Martin lowered his twelve-foot-long lance and aimed it at an Elf which held his own spear up from behind his shield. Still, the old knight having had a lifetime of practice for these moments, and with the skill of one of the finest soldiers Stalwart had ever produced, he skillfully used his own lance to parry the

Elf's spear down then drove the point into his enemy's shield.

His horse at full gallop and his lance pushing forward with a force the Elf had never felt before. Sir Martin knocked the Elf backward with such force his body flew backward into his comrades, knocking them all down, allowing the warhorse to trample them as he passed over them.

Many of Sir Martin's riders behind him never had the luck he did, but almost the entire second rank of chargers did, and the third came in nearly unopposed. The rest of the heavy Calvary's officers recognized the opportunity, changed their approaches, and hit other Elf units, creating even more carnage.

The Outriders, Elves and dwarfs followed them through the lines, got behind them, and began spreading out into their preassigned units and directions, creating the chaos the king had hoped for.

Sir Martin had dropped his broken lance and pulled out his sword, and driven into the neck of an Elf Druid who was trying to create an ignite spell. He laughed again. Knowing the plan worked, he looked back and saw that Eric and his men had quickly dealt with the Elf cavalry and they were already joining the fray. He watched as Eric rode at his best speed to him. With Eric's open-faced helmet, Martin could see the smile on the young Knight's face but then felt a sharp pain in his upper back, and all his strength quickly left his body.

Sir Martin struggled to stay on his horse, fell to the ground where he heard and felt a snap of wood, and realized he had broken off an arrow that had found a way through his armor into his back.

He reached to his head and pulled off his helmet. He tried to breathe and watched as the young Outrider jumped from his horse and raced to him.

"Don't move. You will be fine." Eric knelt at his side.

Sir Martin had been a soldier for too long and knew the young lad was lying to him.

"Get back into the fight, boy!" He coughed with a mouthful of blood and felt himself going. "It is far from over."

Eric cradled him until he stopped breathing, then gently set his shoulders down and moved back to his horse and climbed on. He looked around and found several enemy Elves trying to rally, and took his shield from his saddle and placed it on his arm, then spurred the mare to charge.

27

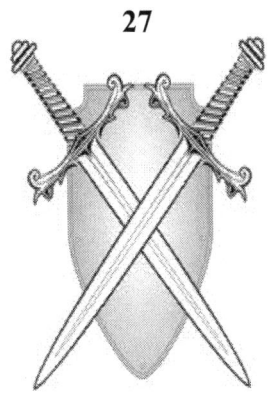

Inda was violently taken from the tent by two of Lirdjss' guards. Inda looked behind and saw her sister following behind and cursing her as they drug her towards a large tree that sat on top of a mound of earth. At first, Inda didn't notice the crowd of onlookers standing in perfect military formation around the mound. She was tied to the small tree that almost all the branches had been cut off, leaving a skinny pole standing tall so as many of the Elves watching could see the spectacle clearly.

The guards attached her hands to the tree high over her head, forcing her to stand on her toes. The white robe was cut from her body, leaving her naked and shamed in front of thousands of Elf warriors. Many dropped their gaze to the ground. A small fire had been lit at the base of the mound and had the end of an iron rod sitting in the flame, getting hotter by the second.

Inda looked out at the Elf army, who were forced to watch, and felt pity for them. She knew most did not believe in the dark Druids who ruled them. Inda knew this was not the way of the teachings their forefathers had wished for their people. She looked closely and noticed a few warriors had tears coming down their faces.

She could hear the battle off in the distance and knew the humans must have attacked. The noise was much closer than the wooden walls King William had his men build. She turned her head towards the sounds of carnage and wondered if Eric was there, fighting for his life, fighting to save her. She wished to see him again. Wished she could kiss his lips one last time, but knew that was unlikely even though Lirdjss had told her their father wanted her brought back alive. Lirdjss had said she was only going to brand her in front of the army. Inda still did not expect to live through this day, especially if the fighting got too close. If the fight was here and not on the hill, the battle might go terribly wrong for her sister's army, and she felt sorry for the Elves and humans that would die this day.

Lirdjss then walked up onto the mound in front of her sister and walked around her naked body, not looking at her but looking at her troops. She then yelled as loud as she could for all watching to hear.

"My warriors, I know some of you have doubted our leadership and have had thoughts of joining the humans against my father. To rally under my sister." She made another lap of the mound before she spoke again. "My traitorous sister who had betrayed my father, the rightful ruler of our people and defected to the enemy." She then smiled cruelly and continued, "Some of you question the power of my kind, the Druid. Well, I am here to tell you doubting us is a huge mistake. We are stronger now than we ever have been." She laughed as she stepped over to her sister. "This is what gave you hope? This weak, pathetic excuse for a Druid."

Lirdjss then turned to one of her Druid followers, who was watching. She pointed to one of her inner circle, a taller male Druid who was there the night Prince Simon was killed and had been gifted his blood. The Druid smiled and walked over to the fire, picked up the iron, and lifted it for all to see. He strolled up the mound, holding the red-hot glowing piece of iron high.

Inda watched him coming closer and stared up at her bound hands, wishing they were free, but realized it was no use. Even if she could get her hands free, she was standing in the middle of thousands of her sister's warriors. Inda relaxed her mind and closed her eyes, and tried to go inside herself to the light and block out the coming pain.

The tall Druid stood directly in front of her. Even with her eyes closed, she could feel him near. She could not see what was happening as many of the army stirred in protest. Some yelled for Lirdjss to stop this madness. The male Druid stopped and looked to Lirdjss, who shouted for him to brand her face. He looked at Inda. Before he could bring the iron forward, an arrow struck him in the back, perfectly between the shoulder blades. He fell to the ground, dead.

Inda heard the thump and opened her eyes, and looked at the dead Druid at her feet. Another unarmored Druid was struck in the chest by a spear that came from deep in the ranks with great accuracy. Warriors in the crowd broke from their ranks and attacked others.

A high-ranking Elf, one of whom was at the parley, began calling men to his side. He already had loyal men around him and started giving orders to attack the Druids. Lirdjss sent balls of fire into the crowd, killing anyone in front of her. Loyal or not, she did not care, but many of the Elves who were attempting to come to her aid did, and instantly changed allegiance on the spot.

A young Elf, only a boy, ran up on the mound, holding his shield forward to protect Inda's naked body. He cut her hands free and gave her his cloak as he pulled her away into a group of loyal warriors who formed a perfect turtle as they walked her out.

Lirdjss and her Druids were killing warriors by the hundreds as her guards pulled them away from the thousands of warriors who wanted her dead.

As the new Elf civil war quickly spread and the numbers rapidly turned for Inda, Lirdjss' people retreated and were directed to go back, closer to the fighting on the battlefield where the humans were attacking.

Lirdjss quickly found herself stuck between two enormous forces, both intent on killing her to survive.

She looked north to the attacking humans, and off in the distance, she saw the young Prince leading a charge of infantry against her own. She cursed at him and knew for her to stop the mass defection of her forces, she would have to kill Prince Duncan and her sister.

28

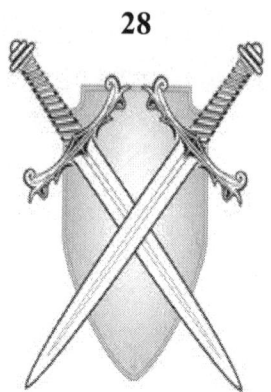

Prince Duncan rushed forward, surrounded by Davy, Brandon, and Davy's handpicked choice of men to keep him as safe as possible. He brought the heavy infantry his father had sent down and the thousands of newly freed men, and they were still picking up more defectors as they advanced, who were eager to join up.

Duncan's men handed out strips of cloth, no matter the color. Anything they could find, and they tied it around their arms as not to be identified as enemies, as the armor they wore was not the standard issue of the Stalwartian army.

Duncan ran forward frantically, looking for Lirdjss or her inner circle of enhanced Druids who killed his brother Simon. As they came closer to the

Elf line of infantry, who clearly had every intention of fighting, he saw many common Druids mixed in with the rank and file. The Druids conjured fireballs the size of Duncan's head and sent them at the human ranks. The Prince raised his hand in the air and easily caught one in the palm of his hand as though a friend had tossed him an orange. He then threw it to the ground.

Duncan then waited until his forces were closer to the Elf line and quickly brought both hands forward. His eyes glowed green as he looked at one of the Druids and sent two small green balls of light no bigger than a hummingbird forward, which shot out like an arrow, struck the Druid in both eyes, and ignited his face into green flame.

The Crown Prince then reached into a pouch on his waist and brought out the two acorns and placed one in each hand, and grew the vines again that glowed bright green.

The Prince's force crashed into the Elf line. The noise was deafening as shield bashed together, swords and spears clashed, sending sparks flying, men and Elves screamed in rage, fear, and enthusiasm as the killing became out of control.

The freed men were the loudest. The rage of centuries of occupation and oppression filled them with a need for vengeance, and they seemed to lead the advance deeper into the killing with no mercy at all. Duncan watched as many wounded Elves tried to surrender but were killed all the same, and not just by the freedmen. The Stalwartian troops were just as vicious. The Prince expected to see this as this was the most crucial battle the continent had seen in five hundred years.

He used his whips like a seasoned soldier. He had practiced with them daily and could wrap them around a neck at almost every throw and pull them closer. Brandon was positioned with his shield and sword to protect him and would cut any Elf down when brought into range.

Often, Duncan would send forth small amounts of mist that would cause the Elves, who came into contact with it, to scream in fear and run away. Duncan reached to the ground, and a moment later, hundreds of vines came out of the earth and trapped Elf feet to the ground, allowing them to be easily killed.

The Druids targeted the Prince with their own spells, but Duncan quickly defeated anything they sent at him. Plus, several paladins nearby would place up protection fields, increasing the safety of the Prince. Soon none of the Elves would come any closer to the Prince, so he was forced to use more of his casting spells and sent green fire into them.

A fresh rank of Elf infantry charged into the field of carnage, and Duncan quickly cast the fear spell and sent some green mist forward, sending hundreds of the once fearless Elves running in panic, screaming in fear. Many of the humans laughed at the sight as they continued their advance—many shot arrows into the retreating warriors.

Duncan looked to his right where Davy was out forward of the rank, engaged with a group of Elves. The Prince watched as the seasoned professional soldier held his shield tight on his arm, his sword firm in his other hand like it extended his arm, and advanced alone on the six Elves. Davy would block with his shield and counter with a sword stab or swing and hit almost every time. It was a sight he had waited years to see and was glad he did. The rest of the humans cheered Davy as he cut the sixth one down, then turned and called for the rest to follow him. Duncan smiled as he knew his trusted friend and bodyguard loved battle like this and dreamed of them.

Duncan sent another ball of green flame forward, opening another Elf rank, and the enemy quickly broke. He looked to his right and could see the Stalwartian cavalry and Eric's outriders. He knew the battle must be going well for them.

Then he had the strangest feeling. He could feel her again. Lirdjss was nearby. He stopped advancing and let some of the men pass by him. Duncan then ran to the right, pushing through advancing human ranks with Brandon behind him until he found an Outrider and ordered him off his horse. Duncan quickly climbed on the horse and could see much better. And there she was, not a hundred yards away, with Lirdjss with both hands in the air.

He watched her for a moment until he saw what she was doing. Off behind her, though miles away, was a thick black cloud. Duncan knew what it was instantly. She had called the birds again, the flock that had tormented the armies at Cyrworth and the relief force from Warriors Point that made their cavalry useless. She had called them again.

"Duncan!" He looked to his right and saw Eric riding towards him, covered in blood that was not his own, using his sword like a pointer and showing him the incoming flock of birds. Duncan smiled at his friend, reached to his chest, and took hold of his crystal, glowing brightly. His eyes instantly glowed. Eric arrived next to him, breathing heavily and with a hint of panic, shouted, "The birds Duncan, she called the birds again."

Duncan smiled and replied, "You did not think I never had a plan for a few crows and buzzards, did you?"

Eric said nothing and kept a watch out for anyone coming at the Prince, but the battle had advanced farther south, away from the position they were at. Outriders and cavalry men came and held their shields up, keeping Duncan safe from any arrows or Druid spell castings.

"What is he doing?" An Outrider with the relief force from Warriors Point asked, "We best be ready to dismount once the birds get here. They attack the horse's eyes, and they will panic and scatter on us."

Eric looked at the incoming flock, then to the Prince who was sitting with his eyes closed. Eric had learned to trust Duncan, and he replied to the Outrider,

"Trust the Prince." He then looked around in the sky's wondering what was happening. When he saw something coming from the forest in almost every direction, it was more birds.

Eric expected them to attack the horses, but they passed over the Stalwartian army and headed for the incoming flock. These were not the crows and buzzards that attacked the military before. They were eagles, hawks, and falcons.

Duncan opened his eyes. "I told you I had a plan for the birds." He then grinned and shouted, "Come, we have a battle to fight!"

Eric looked as more and more of the giant winged predators circled the battlefield waiting for the incoming dark flock, they climbed higher and higher, and when the crows and buzzards came into range, they dove upon them, thus starting a second battle over top of the first.

Thousands of men began cheering for the Prince, which encouraged them to fight even harder. Duncan fought through the ranks again to the head of the advance until everything in his immediate vicinity seemed to stop, and he found himself face to face with Lirdjss, who was less than thirty paces away.

She had four of her Druid apprentices with her. The fighting slowed all around as everyone stopped to watch the magic users face each other. Even though off to the far left, there were sounds and cries of battle raged on.

Duncan dismounted from his horse and stepped forward; dozens of Paladins came running behind the Prince, ready to lend a hand if the other Druids got involved, knowing they had little chance against them. Lirdjss took three steps forward and called to Duncan arrogantly.

"Are you ready, young Prince?"

Duncan shrugged. "Of course, I have waited a lifetime for this."

"I will drink your blood, Prince Duncan!" Lirdjss bellowed.

"You cursed me as a child, killed my brother, who was my hero. You tormented me in my dreams, and now you laugh at me! Believe me, when I say Druid, I am more than ready for this fight!"

The smile left Lirdjss' face. She looked at Duncan like she was trying to figure him out. Eric smiled when he realized she had just figured out that she may have underestimated Duncan. She then chose her following words carefully.

"Was it your idea to send my sister to my camp to distract me? Or hers?"

"Hers." Duncan grinned. "I'm not that smart."

"Yes, you are, young Prince," she snapped. "I was wondering why you did not use your powers more on my army as you advanced. You should have been able to wipe a third of them off the battlefield. You were saving your strength for me, weren't you?"

"Yes, I was. I knew the boys could take your army!" Duncan shrugged.

A snicker came across the Stalwartian ranks, and someone called from behind.

"We are with you, Prince Duncan!"

Everyone in earshot cheered the Prince. The sudden burst of cheers startled Lirdjss, and she took her eyes off Duncan for just a second. Duncan attacked with a quick shot of green light that left his hand and headed at her with the speed of an arrow shot, but Lirdjss was fast and blocked it with a protection field she sent up.

She stepped to her left and sent a long red flame from her hand at Duncan's feet. The Prince dove out of the way, rolled back to his feet, created two green plate-sized shields in both hands, and ran closer to Lirdjss. She sent many fireballs at Duncan, which he deflected with the green shields and sent them to the ground.

The armies on both sides were silent as they watched the battle happen in front of them. They both sent flames and smites at each other, and both blocked easily.

They both realized they would have to close on each other for this to end. Duncan ran at her once again. This time, he pulled out one acorn from his pouch and placed it into his right hand, making the vine grow into his whip. On his left, he brought forth another small protection field, and once the Prince reached his intended distance, he lashed out with the whip. Lirdjss laughed as she dove into a roll and came back to her feet. She reached down to her belt and brought out a small dagger, and held it to her lips, where she whispered a spell on it. Duncan watched as the blade of the dagger glowed red and grew longer.

It seemed like the blade was about to melt; it appeared so hot.

She came at the Prince and swung the glowing red-fiery blade at Duncan's head. He lifted his protection shield up and blocked it quickly. At first, when the edge hit the shield, he felt as though it was an easy block, but then he realized the purpose of the attack. Once the glow red blade struck his protective field, it broke into pieces, and one of the red-hot fragments came over the field, landing against his neck, then slid into his armor, burning his flesh as it made its way down deeper.

Duncan cried out in pain and stepped back while trying to focus on Lirdjss, whose sword grew again. He winced in agony as the Druid attacked once more. She ran at him with the blade up high and brought it down towards his head. He remembered the lessons Davy and Eric had taught him. Instead of blocking the blow, he dove forward into Lirdjss' legs and tackled her to the ground.

Duncan quickly released his protective field in his left hand, brought forth a burst of energy to his palm, and pressed it against her face. The green light burned her face. She pushed him off and rolled away. She quickly came to her feet. Her face was burned badly on her right side. Duncan wasted no time and swung his whip at her legs. The whip wrapped around both her legs tightly, just above her boots. Duncan pulled on it hard and brought her down on her back.

Duncan then squeezed the acorn in his right hand and said a word in an old language. The vine that was around her legs instantly began growing longer and made its way up her legs. She sent a fireball at the Prince. He deflected it easily. She hastily shouted a dark curse at him. A black smoke left her lips and flew at the Prince. Duncan shouted, but one word and a white smoke left his own mouth and blocked the dark one until both vanished.

The vine continued to grow up her torso; she screamed in panic and tried pulling on it, but it burned her hands. Lirdjss panicked, and one of her hands became trapped as the vine continued to wrap around her body. In desperation, she called to her Druids to help her. A male quickly stepped forward but was struck by the smites of at least ten Paladin who were watching. The rest of the Druids, who were watching, stood silent in fear of what was happening.

Eric jumped off his horse and ran closer just in case another found the courage to help her, which two of them found. One brought up a protection field, and another conjured a massive fireball, stepping out of the bubble to launch it at the Prince when he was struck by a smite from off to Eric's left, he looked over to see Inda surrounded by a group of Elves who were obviously protecting her.

Eric lost focus for a second when he saw her wrapped in the cloak of an Elf cavalry man and felt like crying. He did not even know when the second Druid was killed by an Elf who was fighting alongside him moments before.

Duncan's vine wrapped itself around Lirdjss until it covered her throat and head, making her helpless. She struggled intensely to free herself, but failed. Duncan then looked at Inda, who walked over to him. He looked at her with sad eyes.

"I am sorry, Inda, she is much too dangerous to let live." Inda placed a hand on the Prince's cheek and nodded. She turned away and ran into Eric's arms; tears filled her eyes as she hugged him tightly. Duncan looked at Davy, who nodded at him and walked forward and stood over Lirdjss, who could see him with one eye through the vines. Davy looked at the Elf army around him and the remaining Druids, who all looked on, terrified at the power of Prince Duncan. Davy raised his blade high with both hands, brought it down point first, and drove it deep into Lirdjss' chest.

There was silence, complete silence, as everyone looked on as Duncan had his whip withdraw back into the acorn. Members of both armies stared at one another until it was Davy who made the first move and yelled as loud as he could.

"Reform your ranks!" And the mayhem began all over again, but as the humans expected, the Elves retreated. Many dropped their weapons and ran. Others dropped their weapons and held their ground, surrendering on the spot, and taken prisoner.

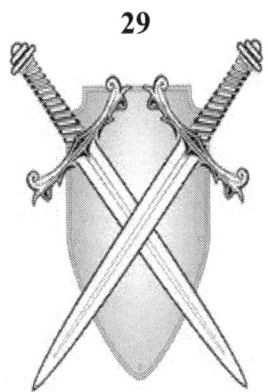

29

Eric quickly climbed aboard his horse and called for his Outriders and other units to follow him. On the gallop, he formed them up and began pursuing the retreating enemy back down the road that would take them back to Cyrworth. His uncle Samuel was beside him, covered in Elf blood from the many that had fallen to his blade.

Most of the retreating Elves made their way into the forest once they realized the human army was chasing them. Eric had his men stay on them, not giving them any piece, and had every intention of running them all to the ground unless they surrendered. The Elf warriors who found the courage to stand and fight were run down like grass by the heavy horsemen who had rallied with the young outrider knight and took pursuit.

After several miles in the thickening forest, the speed of the running battle slowed, and many of the more experienced Elves used their superior athletics and took to the trees where ambushing the human horsemen became easier. Many of Eric's mixed unit, including himself, dismounted and proceed on foot using their shields against the Elf arches, which seemed to put up a highly effective rear-guard defense. His casualties were mounting up.

"Sound the recall," Eric shouted. One man pulled out a metal horn and let out three short toots, two long after. A moment later, Eric heard the call relayed by other men, who did the same signal with their own horn. Eric gave his group of a hundred-plus men orders to form up in an all-around defensive position and wait for his men to return, as he did not want to leave any of them out in the woods alone. His signalman continued to blow the notes, letting his men follow the sound back to him, and quickly, they began appearing out of the trees.

"Here they come, Sir Bowman." A young heavy cavalry man shouted, pointing in the direction he could where the brush was being trampled down under their horse's hooves. "They must be in a hurry."

Eric looked in the direction the young man was pointing. He was right; they were in a hurry. Eric stepped forward-looking towards the incoming noise until he could make out the first of the riders coming towards them. They were not human. They were a unit of heavy Elf cavalry in full charge.

"Mount up!" Eric shouted, and quickly climbed aboard his horse with record speed, as did the men he was commanding. Eric knew he had made a mistake following them this far into the trees and was thankful for the low numbers he had with him at this moment. "Break up into groups and run!"

Eric spurred the mare and galloped away with five outriders with him. He watched as his hundred-plus men quickly broke up into groups and galloped away. He looked behind and saw the Elf unit of over two hundred heavily armored galloping towards them with lances lowered.

Eric continued to gallop, not feeling any fear anymore, and remembered the many times he was being chased by angry Elves after a raid or ambush. He looked at the surrounding men, all Outriders, gave him further confidence. He took another glance behind him and noticed the amount of enemy chancing him had very much diminished and was now less than a dozen. Eric's experience allowed him to calculate the rest of the pursuers must have broken up and gone after the other human groups when they scattered.

"This could be an opportunity." One man shouted, and Eric knew exactly what he was eluding to. He pointed at two of the men running with him and shouted,

"Evade and cut!" Both men smiled and reigned their horses away from the group while Eric and the other three kept their horses on a fixed course, hoping the Elves would continue their pursuit of him, which worked perfectly. After less than the length of an arrow shot, Eric then reigned the horse in the same direction his brothers had left then slowly slowed his horse.

The Elves behind him were gaining, and as quickly as they left, the two outriders Eric sent away appeared behind their enemy with their bows out and were shooting into the Elves' backs and knocked three of them off their mounts before the rest knew what was happening.

The remaining nine pulled on their horse's reins and tried to turn them around to meet the two men who had killed their friends, but once they got turned around, the two outriders simply galloped away and had their backs to Eric three riders accompanying him. The four of them pulled their own bows off their saddles and dropped five more of the Elf, causing the remain four to retreat.

Eric looked up and saw the day was getting late and once again called for a recall to be sounded. It took hours to recall his men, and he brought them back to William's Hill well after dark. He was exhausted and dismissed the men, then reported to General Claiborne and was dismissed for the night.

While making his way back to his tent, he heard a familiar voice in the darkness, "Eric." He turned to find Peacekeeper Rudderham quickly marching over to him with his left arm in a sling and much blood on his uniform.

"Corporal Rudderham, good to see you made the day."

"Thanks be to the brothers alone." Rudderham looked at the green moon over their heads. "I ended up in the middle of the fray near your friend Prince Duncan, bloody scary what he can do."

"That is true," Eric replied. "How is your arm?"

"Oh, it will heal up fine, I guess. A Paladin took the worst of it away."

Eric smiled and placed a hand on the Peacekeeper's shoulder. "That is good, my friend, glad you made it."

The two men said their farewells, and Eric returned to his tent, where he found Inda waiting patiently for him, wrapped in a blanket. He looked at her and walked over, wrapping his arms around her, and kissed her lips. He began weeping as he held her.

"I thought I had lost you." He whispered. She held him tightly, saying nothing, then helped him off with his armor and cleaned him. He lay on the bedroll, exhausted from the day. She covered him with a blanket, then lay beside him until he fell asleep.

30

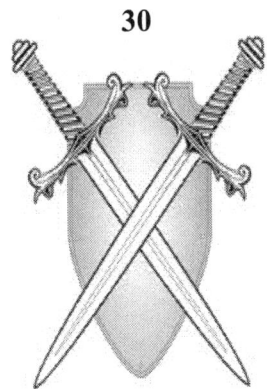

Eric and Inda were both summoned by the King to a crowded tent early the following day. Eric arrived in dirty armor and still exhausted, as was everyone else in attendance.

Inda was dressed in fine light blue robes and kept her composure very well after losing her sister the day before. Everyone in the tent remained excited, fueling their bodies from winning the hopeless battle the day before was keeping them in great spirits.

There were also more than a dozen high-ranking Elves in the room that had defected during the battle. Most had been leading the units that had saved Inda and defected to King William's army.

They were all still dressed in their Elf issue red and black armor, but agreed to wear a white rag tied to their arms to identify them as friendly. They had been disarmed before allowing entry into the tent and had several of Davy's handpicked men standing nearby, watching them closely. Eric could tell as soon as he had seen them, they were very uneasy and stood tightly together in a group against the backside of the tent. Servants brought their plates, of which they all politely refused. Once Inda noticed them, she walked over to them, and her presence seemed to lift their spirits.

The oldest of the newly allied Elf contingent greeted Inda for the group. He had long grey hair, which he pulled back into a pony, and had several scars on his face from many decades of battle. His bright blue eyes made his face light up whenever he was happy and showed his pain when he was in a state of worry. He politely greeted Inda with a quick bow, then took her hand, which she offered him. He held it in both of his own. Eric watched as he said something in Elvish to her, to which she offered him a smile and said something back, and he gently let her hand go. He then walked her around the group of Elves, introducing each of them to her. Every one of them bowed respectively to her, and she took their hands in the same manner and seem to say the same words to all of them.

Gelvyr walked over and stood bedside Eric and watch with him and explained, "They are pledging themselves to her."

"I was wondering what it was." Eric replied, then added, "They are nervous."

Gelvyr nodded. "They have good cause to be, Eric. Five centuries of war cannot be forgiven in a day. The old one is someone I am sure you have heard of."

"His name is General Welloth."

Eric's eyes opened wide, and his head jerked as he looked at Gelvyr and asked in disbelief, "That is General Welloth? The Butcher of Horseworth plains?"

"Yes."

Eric shook his head. "Does the King know of this?"

"He does," Gelvyr answered. "The two sat together half the night talking terms of the Elves joining us in the fight against the empire. I was here with them helping translate as the General's human speech is extremely poor at best."

Their conversation was cut off short when Prince Duncan, sitting in a chair beside his father, eating some bacon on bread, saw Eric.

"Eric!" Duncan shouted, "Please, my friend, come here." Eric walked to the Prince, who stood and hugged the Outrider, then sat beside him. "That was one hell of a battle yesterday."

"It was. We got lucky the Elf encampment was already in such turmoil."

"No. We got lucky Lirdjss was insane and was distracted by Inda's presence." Duncan then looked to Inda with concern, who was still speaking to the Elf contingent, quietly asked, "How is she? Did they hurt her bad?"

"Not too bad. She did not speak of it too much. I think she is hurting for the death of her sister."

Duncan let out a regretful sigh. "Nasty business. I hope she understands why we had to kill her."

"She does. Just give her some time." Eric said kindly.

The King then rose from his chair and addressed the room. His knights and lords began cheering him, and pounded metal goblets on the tables against their own armor plating. King William smiled, welcomed the affection, raised his hands, and calmed them to silence before speaking.

"It was a grand victory yesterday; you all fought bravely and made your King proud!" He shouted, bringing the crowd to cheers again. Once they were calm, he continued, "We lost many good friends but gained many more." He pointed to the Elves in the back who had Inda and Gelvyr translating for them.

The crowd cheered for them, which seemed to bring their spirits up somewhat. "But I am sorry to say this war is far from over. We must push on to Cyrworth as early as today. We must retake the fortress before winter arrives. With Prince Duncan on our side, there should be no problem breaching the gates and keeping our casualties down."

The crowd was silent, and King William knew what they were thinking. They were thinking of taking Cyrworth to take the Elves over four hundred years, and they were going to take it in a few weeks. "Our new allies have agreed to help us in the assault and possibly in garrison's surrender." Many of the knights and lords turned to the Elf contingent, nodded at them respectfully, and then returned their attention to the King. "We finally have a chance to end this war if we keep up the pressure. The enslaved human population, all over the Aethel, controlled lands, are in revolt. Now is the time to attack deep into their lands and recapture the cities, free the people, drive the evil Druids and their supports back all the way to Asari." The crowd cheered for the King again. Even the Elves smiled and clapped their hands, "This war is far from over, but with the brothers' support, it will be over."

31

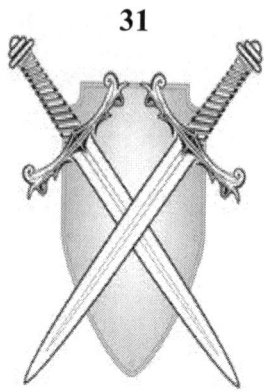

Eric led an advanced group of one thousand Outriders and two thousand Elf cavalry ahead of the army. Prince Duncan was a day's ride behind with his father and the main body of the military. Inda had stayed on the hill with the wounded, hoping to help as many as she could with her powers and kindness.

General Welloth was with Eric, and the two had hardly said a word to each other in the three days they had spent on the ride. They were less than two miles from Cyrworth now. Cheese had been riding ahead of Eric, sending back regular reports of Elf activity. Eric found it strange there were almost none. It had been well over a day since they had seen even a single sign of an Elf scout.

Samuel was beside Eric as they approached the large clearing to Cyrworth when Cheese road calmly up to him and reported,

"There are Elves on the battlements, Eric, and they know we're here, but the gates to Cyrworth are wide open, all of them." Eric pulled his reins and stopped his horse and thought for a moment, confused at the report.

"The Elves would never give up a fortress-like Cyrworth without a fight, never." He paused and looked at his uncle.

"Well, one wouldn't think so." Eric shook his head, then turned in his saddle to Gelvyr, who was riding beside General Welloth. "Ask Welloth if it could be some sort of trap."

Gelvyr nodded to Eric then translated the question to the General, who answered him immediately, translated by Gelvyr back to Eric.

"By the way, the army panicked. He would not be surprised if they abandoned it."

"What about the Elves on the battlements?" Eric asked, and after a brief translation, the General replied, "Possible defectors."

"Possible defectors?" Eric repeated sarcastically. "Well, I guess we should find out then, shall we?" He spurred his horse and motioned for the column to follow him forward. Eric waved Cheese over to ride beside him.

"You checked the forest edge all around the fortress, right?" Eric asked.

"We are good," Cheese replied confidently. "I have men all over the woods keeping an eye open."

"Perfect," Eric replied, then rode at the head of the column, and they moved their entire force into plains outside of Cyrworth and formed up as to not be surprised. Eric then rode forward with Samuel, Gelvyr, and Welloth, holding a horse's tail on a spear high in the air.

Moments later, three Elf commanders rode out of the fortress and slowly made their way for a parley.

Eric chuckled. "I never thought I would lead a parley before a battle."

Samuel laughed and added, "Hell, growing up, you always threw a punch when talking was needed."

They both chuckled, then settled down as the Elves arrived. There were two times in Eric's life where he had sat in on a parley before a battle, and two times the arrogance of the Elves was so strong it made Eric sick to his stomach, but here even before they arrived, he could tell it was a different feeling altogether. He looked at the Elf commanders and tried to figure out what the difference was. He noticed it as soon as the first one spoke. There were no Druids with them. These Elf commanders were their own masters at this moment. They were calm, and even at first glance, Eric could tell they were reasonable.

The Elf began speaking to General Welloth. There was a brief conversation between the two, and the other two commanders seemed to relax quickly after Welloth. Eric looked to Gelvyr, who translated for him.

"They wish to surrender Cyrworth and join General Welloth's forces. The General has welcomed them into his ranks. They said the Druids that were left in charge were going to hold the fortress and fight till the end." Gelvyr listened as they spoke, then reported more to Eric, "He said when the Commanders wanted to surrender, the Druids ordered them killed. There was a battle within the walls between the Elves, and these warriors won. The three Druids who were left in charge were killed."

The commander turned his horse around and waved to the walls. Eric watched as three corpses were thrown over the side of the battlements and landed with a loud thud on the ground below. Samuel let out a snicker at the sight, then controlled himself. The youngest of the three Elf commanders noticed it and smiled at Samuel, and the two nodded to each other. Eric really understood the disdain the common Elves had for the ruling Druid class of their culture.

Gelvyr translated more. "They wish to turn the fortress back over to the King of Stalwart."

Eric nodded. "On behalf of King William Goodwin, I accept the surrender of Cyrworth, but I will not accept the surrender of these men. I will, in fact, accept them into the King's army as part of General Welloth's forces."

Gelvyr translated this, and the commanders smiled in relief and welcomed them to the fortress.

Eric waved his army forward, and the Outriders quickly lined up behind Eric and slowly rode through the gates. Eric could see the damage to the gatehouses where Lirdjss had used her powers to open them. There were dead Elf bodies neatly lined up all over; many were piled high on carts to be hauled out to be disposed of. Eric looked around the fortress. This had been the first time he had seen Cyrworth. It looked remarkably like Seaworth and Rockworth, as all the bastions had been built with the same design but had some minor improvements made over the centuries, making them all a little different.

"Samuel," Eric called out, getting his uncle's attention. "Have our men help with the Elf dead, have them take direction from the Elves as to not disrespect the bodies."

"I will," Samuel nodded, and called for the Outriders to assist him. Gelvyr shouted in elvish for some Elves who were arriving to help as well. Eric dismounted, walked to the outer wall, and climbed the stairs, where he looked out. He could see the remains of a massive battle, most of the bodies had been taken away, but there was still some gear and weapons scattered about and wondered if he would ever hear of the battle in details that brought this great fortress from the human and Dwarves who had held it for so long.

32

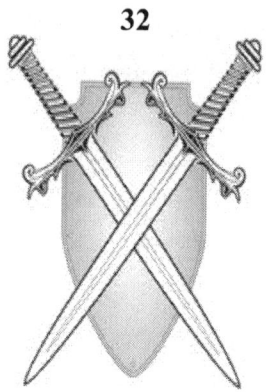

Prince Duncan was lying in bed in the Lord Commander's estate at Warriors Point. He had made the journey to Cyrworth with his father and helped refortify the fortress with a strong Garrison of Elves, Dwarves, and humans, then made his way southeast to Warrior's Point.

Most of the Elf contingent would spend the winter at the makeshift fortification they built on William's Hill. General Welloth said he wished them to stay there where they defected as a new beginning in new houses they made themselves. They used the logs from the palisade to build the base they needed for the winter; King William promised he would provide them with anything they would need for a comfortable winter.

Duncan had been tossing and turning most of the night, as he could not fall asleep. Part of him was still uneasy about the reception he had received after the news had gotten out about him defeating Lirdjss and how he was welcomed into the city as a hero. The strangeness of women throwing themselves at him and offering him their bodies was very new because not that long ago, when he was cursed, most women were repulsed by his presence.

Soldiers and Veterans saluted him proudly and spoke fondly of him and how Stalwart would be in excellent hands once the King eventually passed on and no one would dare call him the Sickling Princeling anymore.

His mother and sister greeted him and his father affectionately, like usual. Duncan hugged his mother tightly and almost had to fight her hands off him as she checked him for any wounds he may have received and fussed over him most of the day.

There had been a grand feast that evening where honors had been given out, and the King ordered his son to receive his ink that night, which he accepted proudly and spent much of the night looking in the mirror.

Duncan grinned as he watched his father grant Eric a castle and lands to the east of Warriors Point, near the border of Krede. He would govern three modest towns and a castle known as Wolfstone, a substantial stone castle with a permanent garrison of fifty men. He could call men to arms from the population all over his lands. Eric would now be known as a Lord and would have to collect taxes from the people and pay a share of them directly to the King.

Duncan had laughed at Samuel, who could not wait to see his nephew's grand estate and pick his own room and demanded to Eric he be the captain of the guard. Inda agreed to come and live with Eric as well, and hinted they were to be married. Duncan shouted she would be the lady of Wolfstone. Eric's father was recklessly proud of his son and bragged relentlessly about him.

Duncan's mind raced and would not stop. He tossed and turned until he sat up in the bed and crossed his legs. He went inside himself and find the light, which always calmed him. Duncan closed his eyes and went in, where he quickly entered the light. He felt the warmth fill his soul and floated around, letting himself go, losing any form of negative energy left inside him. He stayed like that for a time until he heard a familiar voice.

"Duncan." Simon's voice was different. Before, it always had a sense of urgency, but this time it was calm. "Duncan." The Prince opened his eyes to find himself in the green room again, fill with the green mist. He could see the outline of the two tall men standing at the front, watching from a distance. Duncan turned his head to his left and found Simon standing next to him with the armor of the gods and the golden helmet with the single golden horn sitting on his head.

"You have done well, little brother. I am proud of you," Simon said.

"Simon," Duncan choked out as tears filled his eyes, "I've missed you."

"I will always be with you, Duncan. Just go into the light. You will feel me." Simon smiled and let out a gentle laugh.

"I killed her. I killed Lirdjss." Duncan nodded and wiped a tear away. Simon placed a hand on Duncan's shoulder.

"You did, but I am afraid there is much more work that needs doing."

"We will defeat Aethel. I know we will." The smile left Simon's face.

"Aethel and the Druids are not the real threat Duncan, there is a much greater threat coming for Wreten."

"A greater threat?" Duncan repeated in disbelief, "Greater?"

"The book Inda gave you, the book with the green crystal."

"Yes." Duncan reached into his shirt and pulled out the green crystal that he kept around his neck all the time, and held it up for Simon to see.

"You must find the other two books." Simon took off his helmet.

"The other two? I never even knew this one existed until she gave it to me. How do I find the others?" Duncan shook his head. Simon said nothing at first. He simply reached up, took off his helmet, looked at it in his hands, and then handed it to his brother.

"Find the other two little brothers." Simon paused and looked proudly at Duncan, then added, "Alexander the Savior had them." He then pointed at the golden helmet in Duncan's hands. As Duncan went to look down at the helmet, he felt a sharp shock across his body, and he awoke in his bed. It was daylight, and he felt refreshed.

Duncan lay for a moment looking at the ceiling in his room, thinking of the vision his brother had given him the night before, and the frustration came back to him.

"Alexander, the savior, had them at one time!" Duncan said mockingly. "The man has been dead like four hundred and fifty years! Maybe I will just ask him!" He mocked in frustration as he sat up and placed his feet on the floor when his right foot struck something metal next to his bed. Duncan looked at the floor, and his heart began pounding as he looked at the golden helmet his brother had handed to him in the vision. He reached down and picked the heavy golden helmet up and studied it closely. He spun it around and noticed a fine engraving on the backside. As he studied it, he realized it was a picture of Alexander holding three books in front of Paladin Hall. Alexander was dressed in his robes with his crystal around his neck. The engraving showed Alexander reading a book, and his crystal was glowing.

Duncan remembered his trusted Paladin friend, Peter, telling him something back at Warrior's Point when they first discovered he had powers. Peter's voice ran through Duncan's mind as though he spoke to him again.

"Alexander the Savior could not make his crystal glow either." Duncan thought long and hard about everything he had ever read or had been told of Alexander the Savior, and he remembered hearing somewhere the Savior's crystal and sword were still at Paladin Hall.

Duncan leapt from the bed and dressed in a fine pair of pants and a light shirt, then stormed out of his room and headed for the kitchens. He carried the helmet with him. Duncan was overly excited, and he ran down the stairs, down the hallway, barging into the dining room, where he found his father and mother eating a relaxed breakfast, enjoying each other's company.

William looked at his son. "Well, you look like you're on a mission this morning, son." Duncan handed his father the golden helmet and waited for the man of faith to realize what he was holding in his hands. The King looked it over, and his eyes opened wide in shock. "Where did you get this?"

"From Simon, he said there was a danger coming, much greater than the Druids we have faced."

"What does it mean, then? What did Simon tell you to do?" King William shook his head in confusion and looked at the helmet in awe.

"No, please, not again." Duncan's mother cringed, waiting for her son to answer, knowing he would leave soon.

"I must get everyone together and go to Paladin Hall immediately." Duncan smiled at his mother.

The   End

ALSO BY DAN HOPKINS

*

The Third Law Series

***Book 1** : Let it Burn*
***Book 2:** Flames of Chaos*
***Book 3:** Coals of Confusion*

*

The Wars of Wreten Series

***Book 1:** Blood of the Brothers*
***Book 2:** The Battle of William's Hill*

*

Heavens Gate Series

The Holes in Heavens Gate

ACKNOWLEDGMENTS

A special thanks to my beta readers,
Adam, Darlena, and Logan.
Their insights strengthen every story I write.

To my cover designer
Angie at pro_ebookcovers
who makes the most amazing covers.

And
my editor Dawn Baca,
she is priceless…

ABOUT THE AUTHOR

Dan Hopkins was born October 15, 1970 in Red Deer, Alberta, Canada where he lives with his wife Tania, daughter Erica and their puppy Nash. Dan is a former Army Reservist and has been a Federal Corrections Officer in Canada for over twenty years. After he began writing some years back as a hobby, he started to bring chapters to work for his friends and colleagues to read. Enjoying it, they convinced him to continue with the story and publish his first novel Third Law.

You can find him here:
https://www.danhopkinsauthor.com

Made in the USA
Columbia, SC
30 September 2021